this keeps happening

this keeps happening

H. B. Hogan

Invisible Publishing
Halifax & Picton

Library and Archives Canada Cataloguing in Publication

Hogan, H.B., 1974-, author
    This keeps happening / H.B. Hogan.

Short Stories.
Issued in print and electronic formats.
ISBN 978-1-988784-11-3 (softcover).– ISBN 978-1-988784-15-1 (EPUB)

    I. Title.

PS8615.O367T55 2018   C813'.6   C2018-905203-1
                                                C2018-905203-X

Edited by Leigh Nash
Cover and interior design by Megan Fildes
Typeset in Laurentian & Slate
With thanks to type designer Rod McDonald

Printed and bound in Canada

Invisible Publishing | Halifax & Picton
www.invisiblepublishing.com

We acknowledge the support of the Canada Council for the Arts, which last year invested $20.1 million in writing and publishing throughout Canada.

Canada Council
for the Arts

Conseil des Arts
du Canada

ONTARIO ARTS COUNCIL
CONSEIL DES ARTS DE L'ONTARIO
an Ontario government agency
un organisme du gouvernement de l'Ontario

Tara Firma   1

Mr. Gupta Has Had Enough   7

Words for Evelyn   21

A Fare for Francis   43

The Babysitter   51

The Princess Is Dead   59

Empties   67

Louis Remembers   91

Corey Was a Danger Cat   101

Esteem   107

The Mouths of Babes   119

This Keeps Happening   123

TARA FIRMA

TARA LAY ON HER BACK in the tent. The knobby roots and hard, lumpy earth dug into her spine, but she was way too high to do anything about it. She could hear Jim lumbering around in the bush, collecting firewood. There was already a three-foot pile beside the unnecessarily large fire he'd built. The flames quivered and crackled to her left, and made the inside of her blue tent glow green.

There seemed to be a "Jim" at every bush party. That was the mark of a good party—some guy who drank too much or smoked up for the first time and spent the rest of the night crashing through the underbrush, trying to drag felled saplings out into the clearing.

"Yukinever have too mush," he'd mumble if anyone bothered to ask him what the hell he was doing.

Tara knew that at some point Jim, cross-eyed and drooling, would either fall into the fire while pissing on it, or walk right into the centre of it and stand there till he ran back out, screaming and waving his arms, surprised at how much it hurt.

Tara listened to the swell of voices outside the nylon walls of the cheap, three-man tent. She isolated the sound of Darlene yelling about god-knows-what somewhere to the left, by the fire. And down beyond her feet, at the front of the tent, the party was building steadily as people parked on the side of the dirt road that lead to their camp site, or emerged from the bush beyond it. "Planet Caravan" warbled out of a car stereo. The bongos and the mellow, watery guitar were the perfect backdrop for twilight by a campfire. That'd be Dan's doing, Tara thought. He paid attention to things like that, and had rigged up big stereo speakers in the back of his pickup for this very purpose. He'd stand there by his truck all night, playing all the right songs while everyone else drank to the point of chaos or unconsciousness.

Tara could hear two guys arguing about which Metallica album mattered more—*Ride the Lightning* or *Master of Puppets*. One of them said *Master of Puppets* was "a benchmark." He actually said that. He must be a fucking idiot, Tara thought.

The guy labouring between Tara's legs let out a moan and brought her attention back into the tent. Shawn. This guy's name was Shawn. Tara studied his clenched jaw and felt his rapidly thrusting hips, and knew he'd be through in a couple of seconds. She turned her head to the right, and tried to see over the mound of coats and backpacks forming a ridge between her and the other side of the tent. She could see the profile of some other guy bobbing mechanically over her friend Michelle. Tara didn't know the guy. Neither did Michelle.

Dan was over by the cars. He was Michelle's older brother. Tara could hear him whooping it up with Paul, who was sort of Michelle's boyfriend. They were out there telling tales about juvie. Shawn had just come back to town after serving three years, first in a juvenile detention centre up north of the city, then in the dilapidated maximum-security shithole downtown. That's how Shawn ended up at this party with them—he'd met Dan and Paul in the can. Shawn had brought the other guy in the tent along with him.

Shawn stiffened suddenly and squished Tara's ass cheeks in his hands. The meth was wearing off—she felt his nails break her skin. She watched his face freeze in that mixed mask of rage and fear men always wore when they shot their loads. To watch them, you'd think they enjoyed this even less than she did.

He pulled out of her the second he was done, tucked his flaccid, wet dick back into his jeans, and strode out of the tent while he zipped himself up. Tara heard him yell over to Dan for a beer before picking up the yarn they'd been telling, "Those goofs never woulda lasted two days on the inside."

The guys all laughed.

Tara turned to see if Michelle's guy was done. He was gone—must have wrapped it up before Shawn and left the tent. Tara hadn't noticed. She could hear the snuffling sound of Michelle crying, but trying not to. Tara lit a smoke and pulled a couple of hauls off it before holding it out over the backpacks to Michelle.

"Here," said Tara.

Michelle whispered thanks between hiccups and took the cigarette. Tara pushed her hips up into the air, reached down and pulled up her jeans, which had been scrunched around her knees. Then she rocked herself forward and left the tent. She walked over to Dan's truck, where everyone was standing around drinking and laughing. She felt their eyes flit in her direction. They had all been standing there five minutes earlier when Shawn had given her a hit from the smoke wafting up from his foil and then walked her over to the tent for a quickie. Now he stood with his back to her, talking as if he hadn't heard her approach.

Tara's only currency in this group was her edge. She was reckless and people didn't know what to make of that. Some guys liked it. Shawn had liked it. Shawn had matched it. So she knew there was only one play for her to make: she had to dominate the conversation while ignoring Shawn. Give him a reason to try and keep up with her instead of ignoring her. Except she'd already hesitated for a beat while all this social calculus rushed into the space in her head where her buzz had been.

"What do you think of Jim's woodpile?" Dan broke her reverie. He smiled and looked her in the eye, like he could see what was going on in her head. He offered her a beer. Tara turned her back on the group, popped the can with one hand and took a long swig. She looked beyond her tent at the fire and the wall of broken branches that circled the clearing. She could see Jim's staggering shadow flitting across the trees at the far edge of the firepit.

She wiped beer from her mouth with the back of her hand and said, "He'll be in that fire before the end of the night." She held out her hand for another beer and motioned with her head towards the tent. Dan nodded and handed her one.

"Good ol' Jimmy," he said. "Always fucking givin' 'er."

Tara headed towards the fire and stopped at the front of the tent to pass the beer in through the flap. She held it there for a second, then said, "Knock knock." Michelle took the beer but said nothing.

Tara walked around to the side of the tent and sat on the damp grass, facing the fire. Darlene was making out with Michelle's boyfriend on the other side of the fire. Tara lit a smoke and watched them. Paul mashed his tongue into Darlene's mouth and reached down with his left hand to yank up her shirt. He broke off the kiss to suck frantically on Darlene's boob. Darlene stared glumly over his head at Tara and took a sip of her beer without breaking eye contact.

In Tara's experience, guys usually went straight for the main event and didn't bother much with anything like kissing her or playing with her boobs. Paul must really like Darlene if he was doing all that. Sensing his audience, Paul stopped and looked over his shoulder at Tara. He swore under his breath and yanked Darlene's arm hard enough for her to drop her beer.

"Fucker! My *beer*!" Darlene yelled.

"Shut it," growled Paul, and they disappeared into the trees beyond the firelight.

For sure then, thought Tara. Paul likes Darlene.

Tara flicked her butt at the fire and closed her eyes. Her buzz was gone, which left her feeling jittery and annoyed. She could hear more people making their way up the dark trail towards the party, twigs cracking and popping under their high-tops. It seemed like there was too much going on, too many conversations, too many things for her to figure out. She tried to block out all the sounds except the car stereo, which was now pumping "Electric Funeral." The fire burned high and hot. Tara felt the heat on her cheeks; it made her skin feel taut. Her jeans were heating up too, her knees and her shins, almost to the point of hurting, but not quite. It sharpened her focus into an uncomplicated point that obliterated everything else.

Michelle's voice pierced her then, pleading, through the thin wall of the tent.

"Tara?"

"Yeah?" Tara said, trying to keep the edge out of her voice.

Michelle was still crying. Her voice was distorted in her throat.

"I don't know what's wrong," said Michelle, her voice cracking.

Tara bit her lip. Michelle was taking in big gulps of air between her strangled sobs, and it was obvious she was at that point—the point where you start to seriously lose your shit. Tara knew that feeling well but she had no patience for it tonight. She was too preoccupied by the ugly reality of her own situation. No money, no food, nowhere to live.

A backpack filled with dirty clothes, her underwear now a gross mess. Tara usually had no problem hooking up with someone new for at least a couple of days, but most of these guys already knew her and weren't interested. She'd thought it would take Shawn longer to lose interest in her, but she'd miscalculated.

The sound of Michelle's panic, of her struggle to breathe through her snot, made Tara want to punch Michelle's wet, bewildered face right through the wall of the tent. It was such a fucking waste of time and energy—feeling—feeling anything at all. None of it mattered. Tara shook her head and turned back towards the fire. She could sense Michelle in the tent behind her, trembling, leaning towards Tara's shadow, needing Tara to do what she'd always done before. Only Tara could pull Michelle up off the sheer face of whatever it was she was dangling from. Only Tara could hold Michelle tight enough while she cried, could rock her back and forth until she could feel the ground beneath her feet. This time, though, Tara said nothing. Michelle would have to figure shit out on her own. Tara was done.

Inside the tent, Michelle whimpered and bit down hard on the fatty base of her thumb as she watched Tara's silhouette loom larger and larger up the side of the tent, till it seemed to bend right over top of Michelle, as if Tara was using her body to protect Michelle from the screams and the running footsteps that hammered the earth beyond the tent.

MR. GUPTA HAS HAD ENOUGH

"IT'S YOUR TURN, MR. GUPTA."

Mr. Gupta blinked beneath the glare of Abby, the volunteer in charge of their conversational English group. She sat in a folding chair facing him.

"I beg your pardon, Miss Abby," said Mr. Gupta, offering his most apologetic smile. "But I am not sure this story is the right one for me."

Abby sighed and tapped her pen against her clipboard. She wore running shoes, elasticized pants, and a tight top that revealed her muscular arms and back. Her hair was in a ponytail, and at her feet were a gym bag and a takeout cup of coffee. Despite her casual dress, she exuded control, and although Mr. Gupta suspected Abby was the same age as him, he was intimidated by her.

"Mr. Laszlo is your future employer," Abby said. She gestured with her clipboard at Vladimir Laszlo, a heavy-set man in track pants, a fanny pack, and a muscle shirt who slouched in a chair to Mr. Gupta's left. She pointed at the crumpled paper in Mr. Gupta's hands. "Just follow the exercise, Mr. Gupta. Do you need help reading it?"

"Of course not, miss, but I—"

"You're here for a job interview. Mr. Laszlo? Please begin."

Mr. Gupta glanced down at his paper and sighed. This was his first class. His community bridging officer had told him that the government funded these free classes to help new arrivals. He'd been instructed to work on polishing his English, which Mr. Gupta knew meant reducing his accent. His temporary monthly government benefits were contingent in part on his attending government funded classes like these, so that he could prove that he was doing everything possible to gain employment. He fiddled with the lapel of his suit jacket and tried to look enthusiastic.

"Tell me, Goopa," Vladimir said in a theatrical voice. "What makes me to hire you?" Vladimir wiped the sweat from his pock-marked face with the front of his shirt, exposing his hairy paunch. Abby averted her eyes.

Mr. Gupta smoothed his tie with the palm of his hand and cleared his throat. "Please understand, sir," he said. "I have studied and prepared for this position for many years. I sincerely wish to be a member of your team."

"Goopa," said Vladimir, "what makes your Canadian work?"

Mr. Gupta raised his eyebrows and glanced at Abby.

Abby nodded. "Your Canadian work experience," she said. Her pen hovered over her clipboard.

Mr. Gupta frowned and pulled his earlobe. He cleared his throat again and said, "It is true that I have not yet completed this task here in Canada, but I assure you, Mr. Laszlo, sir, that I am eager to do so."

"Mr. Gupta," Abby said. "I don't think your enthusiasm counts as experience."

Vladimir shook his head and looked solemnly at Mr. Gupta.

"I beg your pardon, miss," said Mr. Gupta, feeling a bit hurt. He watched Abby's pen, still poised above the clipboard. "I have not stocked any shelves here," said Mr. Gupta. "But I would not even do so at home. That is for the maid to do."

Abby glanced heavenward as she spoke slowly to Mr. Gupta. "This exercise is meant to facilitate your entry into the Canadian workforce, Mr. Gupta. Tell us how you've done this work, or if necessary, something similar to this work, here in Canada." She bent over and picked up her coffee cup.

"Once again, I must beg your pardon," said Mr. Gupta. "But I am an educated man. This job description is for a stock clerk in a grocery store. I would not dream of applying to a position such as this here or back home, let me assure you."

"Well, there's a consequence for every action, Mr. Gupta," said Abby wearily. "You're not at home anymore, you decided to come here. Please just stick to the script."

"She is meaning," said Vladimir, "Goopa, will you eat shit here?"

"Mr. Laszlo," snapped Abby.

"You insult him with this exercise!" Vladimir bellowed, dangling his dog-eared instructions between his thumb and forefinger.

"Miss Abby," said Mr. Gupta. He secretly agreed with Vladimir's assessment of the script, but he was uncomfortable with the red creeping up Abby's neck and onto her cheeks. "If I may speak, with respect—"

"Canadian shit makes for different eating, Goopa," Vladimir said. He swept his arm in a wide arc, displaying clumps of white deodorant embedded in his armpit hair.

"Mr. Laszlo," said Abby. "If you can't respect our Safe Learning Covenant, you'll have to leave."

"You think I am stupid?" howled Vladimir. "You go." He pointed at the door. "Find script that is help to educated immigrant. I stay here to get my cheque."

"Please," said Mr. Gupta as he loosened his tie. "I will enjoy this dialogue. I did not mean to start a—"

"Thank you, Mr. Gupta," said Abby. Mr. Gupta watched in despair as she stood up, unzipped her gym bag and stuffed the clipboard inside. "Thank you very much for degrading my work."

"I am sorry, please— I only meant that we..." he trailed off as she made for the door.

Vladimir seemed indifferent to the fact that Abby was leaving. He frowned with concentration as he cleaned his fingernails with the arm of his sunglasses.

"Mr. Gupta," said Abby, turning at the doorway to face the two men. "Let me tell you something."

Mr. Gupta nodded eagerly.

Abby hung her gym bag over her shoulder and put her hand on her hip. "The universe will stop giving you these opportunities if you continue to waste them like this." She stood there, head tilted to the side, nodding at Mr. Gupta as though she knew very well what the universe was up to.

"The universe, Miss Abby?" he asked.

"You apply to university?" asked Vladimir, who looked up from his fingernails. "Is good. They have union."

Abby pointed at Mr. Gupta, who watched her, mystified. "I expect more co-operation on Thursday morning." She turned and stalked out of the room.

Mr. Gupta leaned forward in his chair and cupped his forehead in his hands.

"So that is all," Vladimir shrugged. "Is not first time she is angry." He walked over to the card table at the end of the room, used his teeth to tear the corner off a packet of coffee crystals, and dumped the contents into a Styrofoam cup.

"Coffee is shit," he said, filling his cup with hot water from the tap. "But to eat there is cookie. Fig Newton. My wife says is expensive."

Mr. Gupta watched Vladimir fill his fanny pack with cookies from the box on the table.

"I leave some for you, Goopa?" he asked, extending a fistful of cookies towards Mr. Gupta.

Mr. Gupta shook his head. "No, thank you."

Vladimir shrugged, stuffed the remaining cookies into his fanny pack, and left Mr. Gupta to listen to the plastic slats of the vertical blinds tap against the open window. Mr. Gupta glanced at his watch and saw that the class had ended a full hour early. He thought he might go for a walk before heading home.

He stood up and approached the bulletin board that hung beside the window. He scrutinized the flyers and posters and read signs offering child care, private English lessons, carpooling, house cleaning, potluck dinners, prayer meetings, garage sales, and something called Al-Anon, which sounded nice. He ripped off a phone-number ribbon from the bottom of the Al-Anon poster and tucked it into his pocket.

Mr. Gupta peered through the blinds at the park behind the community centre. He saw tennis courts and people tossing Frisbees. He saw a small round wading pool, its perimeter clotted with children in pastel sun hats. Young women patrolled the pool's enclosure in groups of two or three, their complexions noticeably darker than their charges. Under a nearby tree, a shirtless man with profoundly dirty hair strummed a guitar. A woman in a bikini and a brindled, big-headed dog were stretched out on a blanket beside him.

Mr. Gupta stepped out into the hallway. There was no sign of Abby or Vladimir. The lights in the hallway were off, but sunlight streamed through the windows on the exit doors at the end of the hall, and its reflection on the polished floor momentarily blinded him. He squinted and held his hand up to block the glare, and then walked through the rectangle of sunlight towards the exit, his dress shoes clicking softly on the linoleum.

Outside, Mr. Gupta felt the constraints of his alienation loosen. On the south side of Queen Street, he saw a coffee-shop window bearing the logo from Abby's coffee cup. He wondered if he would find Abby inside. Perhaps an explanation of his good intentions, in his excellent English, would come easier in the absence of Mr. Laszlo.

Once inside, however, Mr. Gupta felt even more uncomfortable than he had in the class. The café was cramped, and full of loafing youth covered in tattoos. Music blared from large speakers behind the counter, and none of the children who worked there looked up when Mr. Gupta approached the counter. While he waited for the staff to acknowledge him, he stole glances around the seating area. No sign of Abby, but he did notice a cat stretched out on the window sill and a man fixing his long hair into a top knot.

"Two Americanos, Celeste."

Mr. Gupta started and turned. The man who had been playing guitar in the park was now standing beside him at the counter. He had donned a short-sleeved dress shirt that was noticeably dirty. It was unbuttoned, exposing a torso that was sinewy and slick with sweat.

"For here?" asked the girl he had called Celeste.

"To go," said the man, who noticed Mr. Gupta and said, "Oh hey, did I get ahead of you?"

Mr. Gupta began to shrug it off but the man said, "And whatever my friend here is having." He winked at Mr. Gupta. "I didn't see you standing there. Sorry about that. Go ahead, man. I'm buying." The man held up a ten-dollar bill.

Celeste didn't look up.

The man said, "What'll it be? You want a coffee or what?"

Mr. Gupta shrugged and said, "Thank you, but it is not necessary."

"Hey, make that three," he yelled over the din at Celeste. She nodded.

"Nice day out, eh?" said the man, smiling.

"Yes, yes, it is very nice, thank you," said Mr. Gupta. He began to ease into this small talk. He tried his best to look casual. He pulled his hands out of his pockets, but then couldn't figure out what to do with them, so he put them on his hips, and then on second thought, hung them at his sides.

"This summer has been killer, man."

Mr. Gupta nodded.

"The old lady and I were supposed to get out of town this week but these gas prices blow, you know what I'm saying?"

"Yes, yes," said Mr. Gupta. He was delighted by the ease of this exchange, but he felt anxious, too. He knew that if his accent got in the way, the conversation would become strained, and the man would disengage.

"Yeah, so we might just go down to the lake or something later. Hey, Celeste!" he yelled. "You seen Eric around?"

The woman rolled her eyes. "What do you think?"

The man laughed.

Celeste brought the coffees to the counter and looked at Mr. Gupta for the first time. He smiled, but her face remained expressionless and she busied herself with the cash register. Mr. Gupta directed his gaze down to his shoes. He noticed that the man next to him was barefoot. His toenails were yellow and there was a plain black ring tattooed around the base of each toe.

"All together?" she asked the man.

"Yup. Hit me," he said, and he pushed his ten-dollar bill across the counter.

The cash drawer banged open and Celeste scooped out some change. Mr. Gupta was alarmed to see only two quarters drop from Celeste's fingers into the man's waiting palm. Celeste saw the puzzled expression on Mr. Gupta's face, clenched her jaw and leaned on the cash register. "That's what it costs," she said.

"Dude's got my back," laughed the man. "Watch it, Celeste. He's got his eye on you."

Celeste crossed her arms and glared at Mr. Gupta.

"No, no, no," stammered Mr. Gupta. "I did not mean... I only wondered if... only for three coffees I—"

Celeste cut him off. "It's fair trade."

"Hey, take it easy," said the man. "He was only lookin' out for me, weren't you, pal?" he said, clapping Mr. Gupta on the back.

Mr. Gupta nodded uncomfortably.

"See, Celeste? Give him a break." The man handed a coffee to Mr. Gupta.

"I cannot let you pay for me," said Mr. Gupta. "I did not realize the price—"

"No. Hey, man, hey," said the man. "Relax. I said I'd buy. It's cool."

Silenced, feeling as though he had spoiled their rapport, Mr. Gupta pulled a plastic lid from the pile on the counter and snapped it onto his cup.

"Thank you for the coffee, sir," he said.

The man smiled. "David." He held out his hand to Mr. Gupta. "David Farmer."

Mr. Gupta gratefully accepted it. "Gerard Gupta," he said.

"Pleasure," said David. He took two lids from the pile and snapped them onto his cups. "So I'll see you around, eh, Gerard?"

"Yes, yes, I take class on Thursday also and I would like to—"

"Cool. Take it easy, all right?" said David. He moved towards the door and yelled over his shoulder, "Hey, Celeste! Take it easy!"

"Whatever, Farmer," replied Celeste.

"Thank you for the coffee, Mr. Farmer!" said Gerard, but the door had already swung shut behind David.

Celeste was laughing. "Mr. Farmer!" she said.

Gerard went over to the window. He ignored the cat on the sill, and the cat ignored him. He watched David Farmer trot out into traffic, holding his coffee cups up in the air as he wove between the slowly moving cars. He watched David's head tip backwards as he shouted something into the park, and he saw the brindled dog gallop playfully over to meet him on the sidewalk. The woman in the bikini propped herself up on one elbow and smiled. Gerard watched all of this from inside the coffee shop and tried to recall the last time he had shared such a casual exchange with a Canadian.

He became aware of Celeste clearing coffee cups from the table to his left. He turned his grin in her direction, but she only raised an eyebrow before walking away. Gerard sighed. He left the café and paused out front.

It was humid. The air was heavy and stagnant, and the heat radiating up from the concrete intensified his discomfort. Gerard balanced his coffee on the bench out front of the café and removed his tie. He folded it carefully and tucked it into the breast pocket of his suit jacket. Then he removed his jacket and folded it over one arm and picked up his coffee. He would find his own spot in the park.

Gerard crossed the street and walked east along the southern edge of the park. He imagined that he looked every bit the local, what with his suit jacket draped over his arm and the expensive coffee in his hand. With his left hand, he slid the cup around in his right hand until the logo was visible, but then he realized the label was facing the park. He'd wanted the people passing on the street to see the logo. But by the time he'd figured out how to hold the cup in his left hand so that the label faced right, he'd come to the edge of the park and had to turn back.

Gerard paused and looked around. A street lined with houses facing the park ran north along the eastern edge of the park. He decided to walk up that street, thinking that perhaps the people in those houses might see him as a content Torontonian enjoying his midday walk. They might wonder where he worked or if he was going to stop in to see his family during his lunch break.

The houses in this neighbourhood were tall and close together. Their gardens were choked with flowers, and Gerard saw tapestries, silks, linens, and tassels lining the windows' interiors.

About halfway up the block, it dawned on him that David might know Abby, if they often frequented the same coffee shop, and that he might be able to put in a good word for Gerard with her. David would no doubt see that Gerard was a businessman, and a serious student worthy of Abby's patience and esteem. Gerard was pleased with himself for thinking of this legitimate excuse to speak to David again. He left the sidewalk to enter the park, and walked down around the tennis courts, towards the community centre where he'd seen David sitting with his girlfriend.

Gerard pictured himself acting surprised to find them there in the park. He imagined patting David's dog and meeting David's girlfriend. Maybe while Gerard was standing there with David and his girlfriend, Abby would walk by. He would wave her over and they would talk. Soon all four of them would be laughing as Gerard, with barely a trace of an accent, re-told the story of crazy Mr. Laszlo, and how Abby had erroneously assumed that Gerard shared Mr. Laszlo's contempt for her work.

As he approached the middle of the park, Gerard spied David's girlfriend among the other people loafing around on blankets or tossing Frisbees. He quickened his pace. A few more steps in their direction revealed to Gerard that the girl, still clad in only a bikini, was straddling David Farmer, despite the fact they were surrounded by park patrons and visible to passersby on the street. David lay on his back, smiling up at her. His hands cupped her buttocks. Gerard froze. From his vantage point behind the couple, he saw David slip his fingertips into the girl's bikini bottom. Gerard saw the girl tilt forward, and then she rubbed herself very slowly up and down against David Farmer's pelvis.

Mortified, Gerard held his breath and scanned his surroundings for a discreet escape. He was afraid that any movement on his part might catch their eye. He could not bear the thought of what she would make of a sweaty foreigner staring bug-eyed at her.

He glanced at the people milling about. No one seemed aware of the lust in their midst. Even the couple's dog appeared to be indifferent. But Gerard felt like he'd been slapped. He cast one last embarrassed glance in the couple's direction, and then, walking as quickly as he could without running, he bolted for the north end of the park, across an open field, strategically obscured by the tree under which the couple were undulating.

Gerard was breathing heavily by the time he reached the far side of the field. He stopped to catch his breath in the shade of one of the large maple trees that lined the park. The morning's ebb and flow of tension had worn him down. He did not think he would survive the long walk back to the streetcar stop. The heat, the interminable wait, the damp crush of sweaty humanity on the streetcar loomed in his mind like insurmountable obstacles. Gerard flopped down on his back in the shade of a tree and tucked his folded jacket beneath his head. It seemed to him that above all else, Canadians could not tolerate being misunderstood. Yet when they misunderstood him, and made no effort to try, he was expected to apologize. Gerard sighed, and from beneath eyelids heavy with sudden exhaustion, he contemplated the fluttering green leaves above him.

An ungodly screech tore Gerard, snorting and dazed, out of his reverie. He sat up and touched his cheek. He realized he'd dozed off. In public. Drooling, even. And, to his horror, he had an erection. He pulled his suit jacket onto his lap and glanced around. A dog was chasing a frantic black squirrel. The squirrel screeched again as it raced across the field, headed right at Gerard. He looked around for the dog's owner and saw a figure in the shade of a tree at the other end of the park. A leash hung from one hand, and the other held a takeout coffee cup.

"Charlie!" It was a woman. She sounded more bored than aggravated. "Leave it alone!"

Mr. Gupta squinted, but couldn't see her clearly. He glanced back at the squirrel. The dog had gained ground and was now inches from the squirrel's tail.

"Charlie!" the woman yelled. She stepped out from underneath the tree. Gerard recognized her and jumped awkwardly to his feet, bending slightly at the waist to hide the remnants of his erection.

"Miss Abby!" he yelled, waving enthusiastically.

Abby's face went wooden—she ignored him and focused on the dog.

The squirrel, startled by Gerard, dodged left. The move was fatal. Charlie sank his snout into the back half of the squirrel. The squirrel screamed like a teakettle. Gerard clapped a hand over his mouth and wretched.

"Charlie, no!" Abby yelled, and stomped her foot. Her coffee sloshed through the hole in the lid and she dropped it, watching the hot liquid burble out into the grass.

"Dammit," she said. She licked her scalded wrist while Gerard, who stood only a foot away from Charlie's blood-bath, was assaulted by the sound of incisors crunching vertebrae. In a rapid, wet staccato, Charlie cut short the squirrel's miserable shrilling and gnawed happily on the carcass, his snout turned up towards the sky, his tail wagging.

Gerard's earlier coffee began to rise in his throat. The sound of Charlie's frothy chewing overwhelmed him. Gerard looked away and was surprised to find he was blinking back tears.

Abby stepped back into the shade and fiddled with the leash. Gerard glared at her. For a moment, Abby looked right at him, as if daring him to confront her. He held her eye and struggled to come up with a suitable admonishment for what she had just subjected him to. His lips trembled; his eyes brimmed. He removed his hands from his mouth, clenched his fists and yelled, "Miss Abby, your dog!" He pointed at Charlie. "Please!"

Abby broke away from Gerard's glare and yelled, "Charlie, enough!"

Charlie abruptly dropped his kill and lumbered towards Abby. Gerard waited for her to recoil at the sight of Charlie's blood-soaked fur, to scold Charlie, and to apologize for the mess, but to his astonishment she bent at the waist, patted her hands on her knees, and cooed, "Who's my big boy?" She clicked the lead to Charlie's collar and walked away, ponytail bouncing, the sun glinting off the reflective logo on her yoga pants. Her now-empty coffee cup, forgotten in the grass, rocked slightly in the breeze.

The park seemed unnaturally subdued. Gerard surveyed the mess at his feet. He could make out the crumpled tines of a delicate rib cage. A tuft of fur fluttered forlornly, and a few inches away, the squirrel's once-fluffy tail lay trampled in the bloody grass. He closed his eyes and breathed deeply until the bile stopped burning his throat. In the distance, he heard the chimes of an ice cream truck and the metallic thud of a passing streetcar. He thought of all the people on that streetcar, travelling away from this godforsaken park. Had he not been trying so hard to fit in, he would have been on that streetcar, among those people, his dignity relatively intact.

Had he not been trying so hard. Gerard was was thinking about this when he opened his eyes and saw the opportunity that lay at his feet. He would not waste it. With his jaw clenched and his lips pinched, he bent over and picked up his own coffee cup, removed the lid, and emptied the tepid contents into the grass. Moving quickly, using the lid as a claw, he scooped the visceral squirrel sludge into his cup. He could feel the heat of the muck through the sides of the paper cup. He was surprised but pleased to find it was remarkably light; not too different from the weight of a full cup of coffee. He tapped down the cup's contents with the edge of the lid, then wiped it clean on the grass. He placed the lid back on the cup and ran his thumb around the rim until he heard the lip snap tight. Gerard picked up his jacket and scanned the distance. He found Abby's silhouette at the far end of the park. He knew she would think him responsible for what had just happened. He knew that her sense of entitlement, her expectation of his apology, would make this lesson in consequences uniquely rewarding for him. His dress shoes squelched in the blood-soaked grass as he headed for her.

WORDS FOR EVELYN

EVELYN SQUINTED OVER THE ROOF of the car and through heat waves at the tourists waddling in and out of the doughnut shop. The air in the parking lot was heavy, a tongue pressing down on her head and shoulders.

"Evelyn!" Her mother's voice snapped her back to the task at hand. "For heaven's sake, hold it higher!"

Evelyn straightened her back and repositioned her arms so the beach towel concealed her mother's bent back. The rear passenger door of her mother's rusted sedan was open before her, and Martin, her mother's new boyfriend, lay slumped across the back seat on his stomach with his legs hanging out the door. Her mother, Judy, was using a road map of southern Ontario to scrape the shit off Martin's legs. His soiled boxers hung heavy around his ankles, and the tops of his dress socks were ruddy with excrement. The tableau would have struck Evelyn as comical were it not for the fact that it included her.

"I need napkins or something," Judy said.

"You need a hose, is what you need."

"Evelyn, put a sock in it!" Judy's voice had an edge to it, so Evelyn sighed and went back to staring at the doughnut shop. She felt sure every one of those doughnut-eaters knew exactly what was going on behind her beach towel.

Evelyn said, "You should have pulled over sooner."

"Where, Evelyn?" Judy said. "On the side of the highway?"

"I'm just saying."

"Let me up!" said Martin.

Judy shushed him.

"I need a coffee!" Martin insisted.

"In a minute, dear," Judy muttered.

Evelyn willed her focus away from the car and let it drift back across the parking lot to the highway. Above the whine of speeding cars, a solitary starling tweeted its heart out, oblivious to Evelyn's plight. She closed her eyes and isolated the bird song, concentrating hard until everything else around her disappeared.

Prior to meeting Martin, Judy had been single for thirty-two years. Evelyn's father died when Evelyn was six, and Judy never remarried. The years passed without Judy going on a single date, and she always said she managed just fine with the love and companionship of her one and only daughter.

Evelyn had never dated, either. She lived alone in the basement apartment of a townhouse near an off-ramp just outside Toronto. She kept a goldfish. Its name was Darlin'. She drove from Toronto to Wainfleet every Saturday to spend the night and most of Sunday with Judy.

Sometimes they rented a movie on Saturday nights, but Judy was a fan of swashbuckling epics and Evelyn wasn't, so mostly they just watched TV. Judy would fall asleep in the La-Z-Boy around ten thirty, and Evelyn would poke her with the remote and tell her to go up to bed. On Sundays, they drove to the mall and had lunch in the food court before Evelyn headed back to the city. That's the way they'd spent every weekend for fifteen years.

Evelyn worked as a customer service clerk in the tax department at Toronto City Hall. She hated it, but over the years she had developed a method of going into a state of mental and emotional detachment during her morning commute, and this made her job almost bearable. Her office was a dusty, grey-upholstered cubicle; one in a sea of identical grey-upholstered cubicles. Judy liked to call Evelyn at work a few mornings a week to tell Evelyn what she'd had for dinner the night before and relay what she'd seen on *Dr. Phil*. When Judy called Evelyn at work one day to tell her she'd fallen in love with someone, Evelyn thought she was going to have a stroke.

"Mm-hmm?" was all she could say each time Judy paused to breathe.

When Judy told her that Martin had already sold his bungalow in Cheektowaga so he could move into Judy's townhouse, she smacked her hand down on her keyboard and yelled, "Jesus, Mom!" Her mouse clattered to the floor.

All work-related activity in the cubicles around hers ceased.

Evelyn didn't want her outrage to betray her envy. She groped through her shock for something she could be justifiably outraged about. "Wait," she said. "You met him *where*?"

"Online," Judy said in a sulky voice.

"Like, on the Internet?"

"Yes."

"Like, with one of those dating services?"

"That's right."

Evelyn heard someone behind her stifling the giggles. She heard her mother's monologue in snippets—his name was Martin, he was a seventy-year-old retired electrician, and he was wonderful.

"Does this mean you have a dating profile?" Evelyn shrilled, scandalized.

"Of course, dear."

"Well what does it *say*? Did you use your real *name*?"

"Evelyn..."

"What *picture* did you use?"

"Evelyn, honestly!"

Evelyn held her head in her hands and said, "Oh God."

"Don't be dramatic, Evelyn," Judy snapped. "You should be so proactive."

Evelyn didn't go to Wainfleet that weekend. She expected Judy to call her at work the following Monday, but Judy didn't call. She didn't call Tuesday, either. Evelyn told Darlin' she was looking forward to finally having her weekends all to herself.

Mina stopped by Evelyn's desk one day a week later. Mina was the team leader for Accounts Receivable. She reeked of hairspray, and the horny bent toes sticking out of her high-heeled sandals sported cherry-red nails that looked capable of splitting packing tape. Mina kept up a friendly act, but she was always scoping out whether or not a better conversation was taking place elsewhere.

"Heard the big news about Judy," Mina said, glancing over Evelyn's head at the people chatting by the photocopier. "How's her new love life going?"

"Fine for now, I guess," mumbled Evelyn, busying herself with shuffling the papers on her desk.

"I think it's great that she met someone. You must be excited for her."

"I guess."

"So what about you, Evelyn? When are we going to hear all about a special guy for you?" Mina's eyes levelled squarely with Evelyn's.

"I'm too busy to date," Evelyn said.

"Too busy doing what?"

Evelyn blushed. "I just want to focus on my career right now."

"Oh," Mina said in a tone that made Evelyn feel small. "I see. You just want to be the best clerk you can be, is that it?"

"That's right," Evelyn said.

Three more weeks passed with no word from Judy. Evelyn told Darlin' she'd never felt so alive. No more interruptions at work, no more lame movies, and no more taking care of needy old Judy. On Saturday nights, she rented movies she actually wanted to see, and watched them alone with an air of self-righteousness.

Since Judy's announcement, Evelyn found the gaps in her memory representing her father had been knocking around in her skull. Evelyn's father's name was Dale. Dale Pratt. Evelyn knew nothing else about him, and there'd been no pictures or mementoes of him in their house when Evelyn was growing up. It was an emotionally difficult subject to bring up with Judy. The most Evelyn had been able to cobble together was that Dale had died suddenly due to a terrible and mysterious illness. That had satisfied Evelyn's curiosity up until the day she'd started working for the city. She'd gone for a coffee on her first day with Mina, and Evelyn had provided her usual answer to Mina's usual questions about family. "I was raised by my mom—my dad died when I was very young."

"Oh," said Mina, her eyes growing wide. "I'm so sorry! How awful!"

Evelyn shrugged and sipped her double-double.

"What did he die of?"

"It was very sudden," said Evelyn. She enjoyed being nonchalant.

"Was he ill?"

"Yeah, sort of. It was a mysterious illness."

"What kind of mystery illness?" Mina asked. "Like a cancer?"

Evelyn was now in uncharted territory. She hadn't ever been asked this many questions about Dale before. People usually changed the subject after the "mysterious illness" line.

"I guess so," Evelyn had said. She was astounded at Mina's questions, and bewildered by her own lack of answers.

Mina was floored. "You mean you don't *know*?"

Evelyn shook her head and looked at her lap.

"You mean your mother never *told* you?"

Evelyn blushed and shrugged.

"Evelyn," Mina said, "how can you not know how your father died? He's your *father*!"

Once Mina put it in those terms, Evelyn couldn't fathom not knowing such a thing. She was embarrassed by the way Mina was staring at her. Evelyn knew that look. It was the look you gave stupid people when you couldn't believe how stupid they were.

Evelyn went home that weekend on a mission to find out about Dale Pratt. She was setting the table when she brought it up.

"Mom, what did Dad die of?"

"What?" Judy asked, and the air in the kitchen immediately went brittle.

"What did he die of?"

"Your father loved you very much. He was a warm and affectionate man."

So far, the conversation was a carbon copy of every other time Evelyn had asked about Dale. This is where she usually gave up, because she felt so bad asking Judy questions that Judy obviously didn't want to answer. Judy's discomfort made no sense to Evelyn because, if Dale really was a warm and affectionate man who loved her very much, Judy would have enjoyed reminiscing. Maybe, thought Evelyn, Judy's heart was still broken.

Thinking of Mina, and of how she might be able to save face if she went to work on Monday with more information, Evelyn soldiered on. "What kind of illness was it, exactly?" she asked.

"Your father was a wonderful man, Evelyn."

Judy was beating eggs for their quiche. Evelyn watched her back jiggle. Most of their important conversations were carried out in this fashion—Judy at the counter cooking or cleaning, Evelyn scrutinizing Judy's back for body language that would either corroborate or contradict whatever Judy said. A quickening of the egg-beating told Evelyn that she was pushing her luck.

"You mean, like a cancer?"

"It was very sudden."

"You mean, like—"

"*Evelyn*!" The egg-beating ceased entirely. Judy leaned against the counter and gripped her forehead with both hands.

Evelyn hurried out of the kitchen on her tiptoes and hid in the TV room until Judy called her in for dinner. They ate in silence.

Four weeks after her Martin announcement, Judy called Evelyn at work and, as if no time had passed since their last conversation, asked Evelyn to join her and Martin on a road trip to Casino Niagara. It was Evelyn's turn to work the customer service desk, which she, like all the other staff, loathed. Evelyn turned her back on the lineup of people at the counter and tried to maintain an air of cool indifference.

"It'll be a fun way for you and Martin to get to know one another," Judy was saying.

"But I don't gamble."

"They have a lounge there, Evelyn, with wonderful performers. And Martin really wants to meet you."

Evelyn wondered when Judy had started hanging around in bars watching lounge acts. She guessed it was probably around the same time Judy started trawling the Internet for men.

Judy said, "We can have a drink and watch the show."

"A *drink*?" Evelyn was incredulous. Judy never even had a rum ball at Christmas.

"You know what I mean, dear, you can have a drink and I'll have one of those v-i-r-g-i-n-s."

"I don't know, Mom." Evelyn wanted to say no. She glanced over her shoulder. The woman at the front of the line was leaning on the counter, giving Evelyn the eye. "I can't really talk right now," Evelyn said.

"We don't have to talk. I've told Martin all about you and he can't wait to meet you. Why don't you come down on Friday after work? You can stay over and we'll make a day of it."

"Mom, I said I don't know!"

The woman at the counter sighed and said, "Does anyone *work* here?"

The man behind her said, "Sure as hell don't look like it."

"Evelyn, don't be difficult," her mother was saying. "I'll see you tomorrow night."

"*Mom*!"

Judy hung up.

Evelyn stared at the receiver in disbelief.

"Lord," the woman at the counter bellowed at the ceiling. "I sure hope one day I get paid with tax dollars to stand around yakking it up on the phone. Sure would be *nice*!"

The man behind her said, "Sure as hell would."

Evelyn took a deep breath. "Can I help you?" she said in a flat voice.

"I doubt it, honey," the woman said, turning around to wink at her smiling audience, "but it would be nice if you tried."

The next day, as Evelyn merged with the highway traffic and headed towards Wainfleet, she felt optimistic despite her frustration with Judy. She had realized Judy might have a particular taste for a particular kind of man, and that Martin might reveal something of Dale in their similarities. Granted, she wouldn't be able to appreciate or even recognize those similarities, since she had no impression of what her father had been like. Evelyn had decided to look forward to meeting Martin anyway.

Evelyn pulled up in front of Judy's townhouse and sat in her car with the engine running. She stared at the new lawn ornaments that blighted the yard. An American flag fluttered in the pudgy fist of a gnome at the end of the driveway. On the lawn, a ceramic frog held a crisp brown geranium plant in its smiling mouth. A white plastic lamb in Judy's flower bed strained beneath the weight of a bronze plaque that read *No Bloody Swearing*.

Judy appeared at the front door and scurried down the driveway to meet her. "Sweetie, did you get my message about the macaroni salad?"

"Yeah—Mom, what *is* all this?"

"Oh, it's just Martin." Judy said with a wave of her hand. "Isn't he terrible? Listen, did you stop and pick up the salad like I asked?"

"I said *yes*! But, Mom..."

Judy came around to the passenger side and grabbed the bags from the seat.

Evelyn recalled a fight they'd had when Evelyn was eight and they'd driven down to Florida with one of Judy's bridge partners. Pink flamingoes were everywhere in Florida, and Evelyn had begged her mother to buy one for their lawn back home.

"Absolutely *not*, Evelyn," her mother had said. "Lawn ornaments are for trailer trash."

Evelyn tried to remind Judy of this.

"Oh, have a sense of humour, Evelyn," Judy said. "I've been telling Martin how much fun you are, what a wonderful sense of humour you have—now, don't you go making a liar out of me." She hustled up the driveway, opened the screen door, and called into the house, "Martin, honey! She's here!" She held the door open for Evelyn. Cigarette smoke wafted out past Judy's smiling face.

"Jesus, Mom, is he *smoking* in there?" Evelyn hissed.

Judy ignored her. "Martin is so excited to see you. *Martin?*"

The hallway was cluttered with an unspeakable number of knick-knacks. A stuffed and mounted fish, its gills furry with dust and cobwebs, leaned against the wall. "Are you kidding me?" said Evelyn, pointing at the fish.

"Well, sweetie, it's not fair to Martin if he can't bring any of his things into the house. It's called *compromise*."

A torrent of phlegmy coughs erupted in the den. Evelyn's heart sank as she walked down the hall towards the noise.

Judy got to the den first. "Martin, didn't you hear me, sweetheart? Evelyn is here to see you." She had to yell over the television. Martin was watching golf, and had the volume turned up so loud that even during the quiet moments there was an audible hum.

Evelyn stopped in the doorway beside Judy. A pudgy man with an enormous polyester-clad belly sat prone in the La-Z-Boy. He wore a foam baseball cap and large, clip-on shades that were so dark they looked opaque. There was a rhythmic whistling and popping that Evelyn surmised was his breathing. A lit cigarette dangled from his mouth. The air was blue.

"Evelyn, dear, this is Martin."

Martin gave no indication that he was aware of anyone else in the room.

"Martin, honey," Judy shouted, "this is *Ev-e-lyn*!"

Evelyn stared. Martin didn't move.

"And look, honey, she brought your favourite! Macaroni salad!"

The crowd on the TV burst into applause, and the noise was deafening.

"Are you hungry, dear?" Judy hollered, smiling at Evelyn. "I've got your favourite dish warming in the oven..."

Judy trailed off as she disappeared toward the kitchen. Evelyn pried her eyes off Martin and followed her mother down the hall. She felt sick. She sat down at the kitchen table. Judy was rambling on as she wiped the kitchen counter, her back to Evelyn.

"...and when we got to the deli counter, I wondered if maybe I should try the chorizo sausage instead of the fennel."

Evelyn fiddled with a corner of a placemat and stared at Judy's back.

"And Martin, gosh he's so funny, he says to me, he says, 'Well, why don't you just try 'em both?' and I *laughed*." She paused to draw a ragged breath and then continued, "Because, I mean, chorizo and fennel? *Together*?"

Judy opened the oven door and bent under the weight of a large ceramic casserole dish.

"So then I turned to the woman behind the counter, and she knows I always get the fennel because I've been shopping there for, heck, must be going on fifteen years now! She's the one I told you about, Evelyn, the one whose daughter-in-law—"

More coughing from the den. Judy raised her voice. "Whose daughter-in-law works in the City of Welland tax department, remember I told you? What was her name now, I can't remember..." She stood at the table with one oven-mittened hand on her hip and the other on the lid of the casserole dish. "I can't for the life of me think of her name..."

Evelyn knew the girl's name was Caroline, but she didn't say anything. She watched her mother stare off into space.

"Anyway," said Judy. "Where was I?" She looked at Evelyn. Evelyn looked at her. Evelyn wanted to ask what that hideous slob was doing in Judy's living room. Evelyn wanted to remind Judy of her self-righteous stance on lawn ornaments, mounted fish, and cigarette smoke.

From the den, above the roar of the television: a wet-sounding belch.

"Mom," Evelyn said, "why is he wearing sunglasses in the house?"

"What, dear? Oh, *I* remember—the sausage!" Judy's face came back to life. She lifted the lid, placed it on the counter, removed the oven mitts, and opened the fridge. "So I tried both! And you know something?" She turned back towards the table holding a bottle of white wine and a bowl of greens. "It actually *works*!" She laughed and put the wine and the greens on the table beside the casserole dish and the macaroni salad, then spun around to open the cutlery drawer.

"You bought wine?" asked Evelyn.

"Yes," Judy said, rummaging for the corkscrew. "I thought we'd celebrate." She found the corkscrew and reached up into the cupboard for wineglasses.

"Celebrate what?"

Judy handed Evelyn the corkscrew. "You'll have to open it, dear," Judy said. "I can never manage those things."

Judy pulled her chair up to the table and sat down with a contented sigh.

Evelyn hadn't moved.

"What's the matter, did I not get you a glass?" Judy made a move to get up.

"No, Mom. Just sit. I've got one."

"Well, then what are you waiting for, silly? Open the wine!"

"Isn't he going to eat with us?"

"Who, *Martin*?" Judy laughed and made a face. "No, honey, Martin eats his dinner in front of the TV. I'll fix him a plate when we're done." Judy reached for the salad. "These greens are those organic greens that you buy in the big plastic containers? You know the ones?"

"You let him eat in front of the *TV*?"

"Oh, for heaven's sake, Evelyn, honestly!"

Evelyn took a deep, uneven inhale and sighed.

Judy placed her fork on her plate and dabbed at her mouth with her napkin. "Evelyn, honey." Her voice was quiet but firm. "Martin is a wonderful man."

The silence between them seemed to draw the roar of the television down the hall and into the kitchen. Evelyn stared at her plate.

"These greens really are lovely," Judy said, her voice back to its brusque, clipped tone. "Have you tried these before? I forget the brand name, but I'm sure you could find something similar in the city..."

More coughing from the den. Evelyn reached for the wine.

They left for the casino the next morning, right after breakfast. Judy drove because Martin was on migraine medication that prevented him from driving, although Evelyn noted that he was apparently still free to smoke cigarettes and suck back coffee from a Thermos. Evelyn sulked in the back seat.

After ten minutes on the highway, Martin fell asleep with his head pressed against the door, and his whistling and popping became groaning and choking.

"How does a man who drinks that much coffee fall asleep at ten a.m.?" she whispered at Judy.

Judy clamped her lips into a tight line and gave Evelyn a stern look in the rear view mirror. "I hope people are more understanding with you when *you're* a senior citizen."

"It's a valid question, Mom. He's had about three pots of coffee."

"Evelyn, please!" Judy hissed. "Keep your voice down!"

Evelyn flung herself back in her seat and glared out the window.

"I think maybe someone got up on the wrong side of the bed this morning," Judy whispered. "That's what I think."

"I think that's some crazy migraine medication, that's what I think."

"Young lady!"

Evelyn crossed her arms and slouched.

Judy read out loud the signs they passed. "Speed kills." She laughed. "Well, you've got that right!" She smiled and winked at Evelyn in the rear view mirror. Evelyn rolled her eyes.

Evelyn had only one memory of her father. Or rather, she suspected it was a memory of her father, but the circumstances that unearthed the memory were such that Evelyn knew better than to ask Judy if she was right.

The memory came to her one February morning when she was on her way to work. It was early enough that it was still dark outside. She stopped to use a bank machine and saw a homeless man asleep on the floor inside the vestibule. A grimy baseball cap lay upside-down on the floor beside him. Someone had tossed in a crumpled five-dollar bill. Evelyn hesitated with her hand on the door, but when she stuck her bank card in the slot and the door buzzed, the man didn't stir. Evelyn figured he was unconscious and wouldn't be any trouble, so she pulled open the door and walked into a solid wall of stench. It was a mixture of urine, body odour, and the sharp musk of booze leeching through sweaty, unwashed skin. It stopped Evelyn in her tracks, door in hand, and made her throat close.

As she stood there trying to force air back into her lungs, Evelyn very clearly recalled being rocked to sleep in the arms of a man who was humming a lullaby with his lips pressed against her hair. She could feel the warmth of his breath on the top of her head, and the hair on his forearms against her cheek. She felt her body relax, and a wave of blissful sleepy-headedness washed over her so that she had to grip the door frame of the vestibule. A gust of frigid air blasted in through the open door and the homeless man's five-dollar bill scuttled across the tile floor. He raised his swollen, dirty face and let loose a stream of obscenities that snapped Evelyn out of her reverie. She gasped and stepped backwards out of the vestibule, letting the door close, her mittened hands clamped over her mouth.

Evelyn was revisiting this memory in the back seat of Judy's car when Martin snorted awake from his nap.

"I need the bathroom," he said.

Judy glanced over at him. "You're awake!"

Martin said, "I need to go."

"In a minute, dear, there's a truck stop with a doughnut shop just a couple of miles ahead."

"Now!"

"I said in a minute, dear."

Evelyn saw him dig his nails into window ledge of the car door. "Mom, maybe you should speed up."

"I'm already doing two kilometres over the speed limit, Evelyn."

"I think he really needs to go."

"I'm quite aware of the situation, thank you very much."

"Well then, why don't you—"

"*Evelyn*!"

"Whoopsie-daisy," Martin said.

Evelyn and Judy were silent.

"Whoopsie-daisy," Martin said again, louder this time.

"Oh my god," Evelyn said.

"Martin," Judy said. "Have you had an accident?"

"I told you," he said.

"Oh my god." Evelyn held one hand over her nose and mouth and lowered her window with the other.

Judy tightened her grip on the steering wheel. When she'd sped up by another five kilometres, she snapped off the radio so she could concentrate. They drove on in silence, wind thundering through the open windows, hair whipping their cheeks. Martin held his ball cap on his head with one hand and clutched the car door with the other.

When they pulled into the crowded truck stop, Judy slowed down in the row immediately in front of the dough-nut shop, looking for a spot.

"What are you doing?" Evelyn yelled. "You don't have time to look for a spot—just park!"

"Well, I don't want to walk in this heat."

"Jesus, Mom, just park the car, will you?"

"Just park," said Martin.

Judy let out a tight sigh and drove straight to the back row, where there were plenty of spots. Judy pulled into one, and Evelyn flung her door open before Judy had shut off the engine.

"Evelyn," Judy yelled. "You can wait until the car has stopped!"

"I'm out of here."

"You can wait for us!"

"For what?"

"Just wait!"

Martin was fumbling with the car door and trying to pull himself out. Judy hurried around to the passenger side to help him. Evelyn stood behind the car, facing the doughnut shop with her arms crossed. She wanted to disappear.

"Oh, dear," Judy said. "Oh, Martin, I'm so sorry."

Evelyn shook her head so that her hair hung down on either side of her face.

"Here," Judy said to Martin. "Let's see if we can get you cleaned up first." Judy held open the back door and helped ease Martin into the seat. "Just lie down, sweetheart."

"God, Mom, can't you just take him to the *bath*room!"

"Evelyn, he can't do this alone, and I can't go in there with him. Can you stop being so self-centred for once in your life and just help us!"

"He's *your* boyfriend—*you* help him. I'm going for a walk." Evelyn started to walk away.

"*Evelyn!*" Judy yelled so loud that there was an echo off the concrete, and some of the people milling around the front of the shop looked in their direction. Evelyn froze.

Judy stood up, planted her hands on her hips, and glared over the roof of the car at Evelyn. "I cannot believe how childish you're being. You are a grown woman, Evelyn!"

Evelyn looked down at the pavement.

"There's a towel in the trunk. Bring it over here and hold it up around me. I want to clean Martin up so he can at least walk inside with some dignity." Judy bent back down and Evelyn heard Martin's belt buckle jingle. She wanted to run, but instead she sighed and popped open the trunk.

When Judy had done what she could with the road map, she walked over to the doughnut shop to steal a roll of toilet paper from the restroom. That left Evelyn alone with Martin, who was in an excessively awkward position. Evelyn held the beach towel aloft and stared at the cars out on the highway.

"Let me up," Martin demanded in a wobbly voice.

"Who's stopping you?"

"Where's Judy?"

"She's in the bathroom."

Martin considered this. Then he said, "I didn't mean to end up like...for it to happen like this."

"What do you mean?" Evelyn felt nervous. She didn't like how Martin was suddenly earnest and communicative. "You mean how you made a mess?"

"Yeah."

She wanted him to stop talking.

Martin kept at it. "I didn't mean for any of this to—"

Evelyn cut him off. "Never mind!"

"I tried to do the right thing, but I just—"

"Try harder next time, will you?" Evelyn said.

"I did try."

"Well, try harder."

Evelyn was relieved to spot Judy picking her way around the cars. Evelyn watched her and thought about how Judy so rarely lost her temper or faltered in her cheery act. After all the years and all the loneliness she must have felt, she was still always plucky and determined. Evelyn thought it a shame that Judy had made all that effort to remain upbeat in order to end up here, like this, with Martin. She wished she could be proud of her mother, but instead, watching her stride purposefully towards the car with a roll of toilet paper tucked under her arm, Evelyn felt only disappointment and pity.

"Everything okay here?" Judy asked.

Evelyn dropped the beach towel. "You tell me," she said. "Does it look okay to you?"

Judy pursed her lips and stepped past Evelyn. Evelyn raised the beach towel up again and went back to watching the cars on the highway.

"Here, sweetheart," Judy murmured. "We're almost done."

"Judy?" Martin warbled. "Judy, I can't."

"Sh-sh-sh," Judy whispered. "You're going to be fine, Martin."

"I don't...I can't do this!"

"Just don't think about it, darlin'. Right now, we've just got one thing to deal with, and that's this, and I'm helping you. One thing at a time. Okay? We're almost done."

Evelyn had heard that very same speech from Judy innumerable times growing up. All the nights Judy sat up with Evelyn at the kitchen table until way past bedtime so that Evelyn could practice her multiplication tables. It made Evelyn sick to hear Judy use those words—*Evelyn's* words—on that horrid mess of a man.

"I tried to tell her, Jude," Martin was crying.

"Oh, Martin, not now..."

"I tried to tell her—"

"Martin, *stop it*!" Judy snapped. Her hands were shaking as she pulled Martin's pants from the car door and fed his limp, bare feet through the leg holes. His socks were in a ball beneath the car with his underwear. "Now roll over and pull up your pants."

Martin heaved and grunted. The car shook. Judy straightened up and turned to Evelyn. Evelyn looked down and busied herself with folding the beach towel. "Let's go if we're going," she said. She walked around to the open trunk and tossed in the towel.

"I need my coffee," Martin said.

"All right, Martin. Enough," said Judy.

Evelyn recognized the opportunity to escape. "Fine," she said, walking towards the driver's-side door so she could reach his Thermos. "How does he take it?"

She stood up and turned the Thermos over in her hand. Some of the letters had worn off.

Dale M. Pr t ectrical—We ight up y r life

"Tell them to fill it up only halfway," Judy was saying. "He takes it black."

There was a ringing in Evelyn's ears that made everything sound far away. Her scalp felt tingly. She walked away without a word, gripping the Thermos so tightly that the skin on the back of her hand felt like it would split. She didn't ask if Judy wanted anything, and she didn't care. Evelyn knew Judy would say, "No, thank you," even though she really wanted a cruller. Evelyn knew that the Thermos would stink of booze even though Judy would insist that it didn't. Evelyn knew everything, and she thought it ironic that this should feel as though she was losing her mind.

The kid behind the counter jerked his head back and wrinkled his nose at the smell of the Thermos. He eyed Evelyn over his shoulder as he poured the coffee.

"Is that everything?" he asked warily as he handed her the half-full Thermos.

"Sure as hell better be," said Evelyn. She tossed the money on the counter, slapped the lid on the Thermos, and walked out of the doughnut shop towards her family.

A FARE FOR FRANCIS

THE SLIDING GLASS DOORS of the arrivals terminal whirred open and a young woman tottered out on impossibly high heels. Francis watched her through the freshly washed windshield of his cab. She paused for a moment and fiddled with her BlackBerry, and then smiled as she turned towards the taxi stand. Francis glanced at his rear view mirror. He groaned when he saw there were no other cabs behind him.

"For crying out loud," he muttered as he shoved his half-eaten lunch back into the lunchbox on the passenger seat and sucked the potato chip salt off the yellowed ends of his moustache. He could see that he'd been driving his cab longer than his prospective passenger had been living. Her bright white suit and oversized sunglasses were irritating. Nobody dressed like that in Thunder Bay.

The woman bent over and placed her hand on the open passenger window.

"Hi, there," she said, smiling.

Francis eyed the finger prints she was leaving on the car door and stabbed at his Slurpee with his straw.

She said, "Can you take me downtown?"

"S'pose so," Francis said.

She opened the back door and tossed in her huge purse and flopped down beside it. Francis cringed as she slammed the door shut. Then she just sat there, smiling expectantly at him.

"So?" Francis said.

The woman ran her fingers through her blonde hair. She said, "So!"

Francis said, "So are you gonna tell me where we're goin'?"

"Oh, right," she laughed, and shook her head. "It's downtown, but, um..." She extracted her BlackBerry from her pocket and poked at it with her thumb.

Francis sighed.

"Right," she said. "Here we go. Eighty-six Cumberland Street South." She looked up at him and furrowed her brow. "Do you know where that is?"

Francis rolled his eyes. "Yah, I know where it is." He watched her face in his mirror and said, "Port Arthur."

"N-no," she said, checking her BlackBerry. "It's in Thunder Bay."

"You're going to Nishnawbe-Aski Legal Services."

"Yes, that's right!" she exclaimed, amazed.

"I got this, ma'am," said Francis. "Just relax."

"Fantastic." She sat back in her seat and grinned out her window at the trees.

"That's quite the paint job you've got," she said.

Francis didn't feel like talking to her about it, so he pulled the cab away from the curb in silence. He'd bought his used '94 Caprice 9C1 a few years back from a guy who refurbished them for the police. The body was white, but the hood, doors, and trunk had to be repainted. He'd done them in Neptune Green. Same colour as his old man's prized possession, a '55 Chevy Bel Air that was still in mint condition in Francis's garage. The family heirloom. Had his dad lived to see it, he would have gotten a real kick out the Caprice's paint job. This woman wouldn't know the first thing about any of that.

"I can't believe how clean the air smells here," she said, indifferent to Francis' silence.

Francis rolled his eyes.

"I mean really," she said. "In Toronto, if you can breathe there at all, you regret it immediately."

Francis turned onto the highway. "Yeah, well, welcome to Thunder Bay." He was being sarcastic, but she seemed touched by the sentiment.

"Thanks!" she said.

They drove in silence for a little while. The woman looked every which way, as if there was something to see besides grass and trees.

She said, "So, have you lived here long?"

"Yup. And my parents before me, and my grandparents before them."

"Huh," she said, nodding. "I take it you like it here, then."

"I guess so."

She said, "Well, it sure smells good."

"Mm-hm," Francis said, he watched her face in his rear view mirror. "Used to be a beautiful place till the Indians took over."

The woman's smile stiffened. Francis smirked and sipped his Slurpee. He had her pegged.

"That's right," said Francis. He turned down the talk radio so he didn't have to shout over it. "I got nothing against Indigenous, or First Nations, or whatever they want to be called these days," he said.

"You could just ask which band they're—"

"Well, maybe they should make up their minds," he snapped. "Don't get me wrong," Francis continued. "There's some that's good people. Like ones who got pride in their culture, and their homes and whatnot. But all's the drunk ones do is wreck the scenery."

Francis paused, but the woman said nothing.

They were driving down a rural highway that passed momentarily through an old subdivision. Francis glanced in his rear view mirror and saw that the woman was chewing her bottom lip and frowning out the window.

"You'll see. They're all over the place downtown."

The woman's lips worked to shape the words that failed her. Francis craned his neck to see what she was looking at.

He saw old Bobby Hamilton at the top of the steep incline that was his front lawn. Sweat and grass darkened the front of his CNR baseball cap. He wore a white undershirt that strained to contain his belly, and balanced on the top of his belly, wedged between his breasts, though it wasn't yet noon, he cradled a Labatt 50 protected by a Styrofoam cozy. His pale, spindly legs protruded from his walking shorts and terminated in black dress socks and orthopedic shoes. Bobby had decided years ago that his heart couldn't take the walk up and down that steep front yard of his with the weight of his lawn mower, so he'd tied a length of bright yellow rope to the mower's handle and now stood stationary at the top of his hill, easing the mower down by slowly letting out the coils of rope that lay at his feet. His shoulders and chest were bright pink with sunburn. Bobby spotted Francis's cab and raised his beer cozy in a wobbly salute.

"Shit," Francis muttered as he looked back at the road.

The woman was excited. "You know that guy?" she said.

"Yeah, I know him," Francis mumbled.

"He's hilarious!" she crowed as she turned in her seat to watch Bobby through the rear window.

"That ain't nothin'." Francis was annoyed. "Just Bobby being Bobby." He tried to regain his momentum. "Listen, I got nothing against Toronto," he said. "I just don't like how they spend all our taxes on their roads and that damn duck in their harbour. Meanwhile, the Indians are saying we can't even celebrate Canada 150 because—"

"Okay, look," the woman said. She turned back around and met Francis's eyes in the rear view mirror. Her face was solemn. "Why don't you just drop me off here and I'll walk the rest of the way."

"You want to walk?" Francis said.

"Sure. Enjoy the scenery."

"There's not much to see unless you like looking at drunk Indians."

"It's a nice day out," she said. "You can let me out here."

Francis shook his head. This woman's refusal to take his bait was getting to him.

"Another problem," he said with renewed enthusiasm, "is all them kids raised by single moms. They mess it up for everyone, you know. Single mothers." He glanced at her in the rear view. She was scowling.

"Women just keep on having kids so's they can get more welfare and child support and benefits. It's true," he said, catching her eye and nodding. "I hear them say it again and again right here in my cab. They have as many kids as they can so's they don't have to work, and men are left paying for it all, and I think they should all just—"

"Where do they get the sperm from?" the woman said.

Francis nearly drove off the road. "Wh–what now?"

"These calculating destroyers of worlds. Tell me—who ejaculates in them?" She'd gone pale and was clutching her bag to her chest.

"How the hell should I know, lady?" Francis said. "Jesus Murphy, I never—What do you—I just..." His train of thought abandoned him, so he adjusted his baseball cap.

"These women don't just spontaneously fertilize themselves," the woman said. "You are aware of that biological reality, are you not?"

"Look, simmer down!" He turned the talk radio back on to try and drown her out. The collar of his T-shirt felt tight.

"Let me out of the car," the woman said.

Her voice was so quiet that Francis was tempted to act as though he hadn't heard her.

"Let me out now!" The woman said it louder this time. A muscle at the side of her mouth twitched.

"You can't walk from here," Francis said. "You're too far away from the—"

The woman shot forward in her seat so that her mouth was inches away from Francis's ear. She smelled like the big pink flowers his wife always cut from the bushes beside the porch and stuffed into vases around the house until the place reminded him of a funeral parlour.

"Listen to me, fuckwit," she said in a low voice.

Francis swallowed.

"You pull the cab over this second or I'll make you sorry you ever set eyes on me."

"Lady, let me tell you—I'm already sorry!"

"Have I made myself clear?" she said. She threw a twenty into the front seat. The meter was at twelve.

Francis pulled over more out of shock than obedience. He was afraid that if he looked at her, his bulging eyes would betray his surprise, so he kept his stunned gaze locked on the shoulder just beyond his front bumper. He had barely slowed down before the woman flung open her door.

"Whoa," yelled Francis, as he slammed on the brakes. His Slurpee sloshed forward and his lunch box shot off the passenger seat and onto the floor. She slammed the door and was off, wobbling right down the gravel shoulder of Highway 61 in her high heels, her massive purse tucked up under one arm while the other pumped back and forth.

He pulled up beside her and hollered out the passenger window, "Hey! It's too far to walk from here!"

She ignored him.

"Hey!" Francis tried one last time, but she refused to even look at him.

Francis reluctantly picked up speed and drove away. He shook his head and straightened his baseball cap as he eyed her diminishing figure in his rear view mirror. When she was just a speck on the horizon, he lifted his foot off the gas pedal. He was sure she'd change her mind and wave him back at the very last second. Francis was prepared to pick her up again, despite all the crazy stuff she'd said. He was a reasonable man. But the woman didn't wave, and then she was gone, hidden by the horizon.

"Honestly," said Francis as he pressed his foot back down on the gas. He swirled what was left of his Slurpee and thought about the things she'd said. Like sperm, as though it were just a word. In thirty-eight years of marriage, despite having had four boys and all of the awkward moments that came with trying to raise them up to be decent in a world that had continually disappointed Francis, his wife had never, ever had cause to utter the word sperm. He didn't know what to make of it. The woman's perfume lingered in the car, and he could still feel how her breath had tickled his neck when she'd hissed in his ear. Her voice, when she was angry, had been deeper and quieter than that of any woman he'd ever heard.

Francis slowed down, looked over his shoulder to check his blind spot, and then made a U-turn, palming the steering wheel and poking at his moustache with the tip of his tongue. He'd just drive back and see. If she'd cooled off, he could convince her to get back in his cab, and maybe they could have a good-natured debate. He smiled when he saw the woman's solitary silhouette pop up on the horizon.

The woman, who had removed her heels and rolled the cuffs of suit jacket, glanced up from her BlackBerry and saw the cab had reappeared in the distance. She swore under her breath, tucked her phone into her pocket, and shoved her Blahniks into her purse. Then she squatted down at the side of the road and, with trembling, manicured hands, collected the largest chunks of gravel she could find.

THE BABYSITTER

RUTH, TEN, SAT AT THE KITCHEN TABLE, chewing on her straw and avoiding Mandy's eyes. Mandy was her fourteen-year-old neighbour, which made her practically an adult in Ruth's eyes. The kitchen they were in was not Ruth's or Mandy's. They were in the house of the kids Mandy was babysitting. The Cheswicks. Mandy had given Ruth a tall green Tupperware cup filled with flat orange pop. Mandy then poured some Crystal Light into a wineglass for herself and leaned back against the Cheswicks' kitchen counter with her hips slung forward in a way that made Ruth feel small.

The Cheswick house was cool and dark despite the blinding white heat outside. The air conditioning felt sharp on Ruth's sweaty skin and raised goosebumps on her arms and legs. The carpet in the hallway was brown, the kitchen linoleum was beige, and the textured wallpaper a deep, mossy green. All of this colour seemed to absorb any sunlight that fought its way through the green curtains that hung heavy with dust over each window.

"So, like," said Mandy, shifting her weight from one leg to the other with a slow, sideways sweep of her pelvis, "d'you ever babysit?"

Ruth fidgeted. She had a feeling that looking after her kid sister Sara for half an hour after school didn't really count. She'd already signed up for the St. John's Ambulance course being offered over the summer, but she felt as though it was imperative that Mandy not know how badly Ruth wanted to do what Mandy had been doing for ages now.

Mandy didn't wait for an answer. "I been doin' it for ages now."

Ruth tried to look as though she wasn't interested. She pulled back from her plastic cup and watched as the line of spit between the straw and her lips got thinner and thinner, until it broke and fell across her chin. There were molar marks on her straw. She wiped her chin, put the straw back in her mouth, and resumed chewing.

"I musta babysat practically every kid on this block," Mandy sighed.

"You never babysat us!" piped up Sara, who stood at the entrance to the kitchen with her pudgy hands on her hips.

"We don't *need* a babysitter, Sara!" Ruth snapped.

She turned back to Mandy and declared, "We don't need a babysitter."

Mandy shrugged and swirled her wineglass. "I really like babysitting. Except for these shits." She jutted her chin out towards the hallway leading to the back of the house. "They're a handful."

Ruth nodded. Brandon and Wayne Cheswick were the worst kids on their street. They played rough and stole marbles, but Ruth chose not to share this with Mandy. She didn't want Mandy to know that she still played marbles, because she suspected Mandy never played with kids who needed a babysitter. Ruth could hear the Cheswicks in the backyard, screaming and thumping something heavy against the side of the house. Sara, who was younger than the Cheswicks and was therefore often the first victim in their games of capture the flag or kick the can, looked over her shoulder, down the hall towards the thumping noise, eyes wide, thumb in her mouth.

"I'm *so* glad we're friends again, Ruth," Mandy said, her voice suddenly warm with inexplicable affection. "I really like catching up with you like this."

Ruth smiled thinly around her straw. Mandy talked like a grown-up on TV. Ruth didn't know whether to be impressed by that or not. Ruth's mother once said that Mandy was best left alone because she was "trouble."

It had been six years since the last time Mandy had shown any interest in Ruth. Back then, Ruth and her family had just moved to Dibgate Crescent. Ruth and Sara were in their backyard, playing in the sandbox at the side of their house, under the kitchen window. Sensing they weren't alone, Ruth had looked up to see Mandy's face wedged between the boards of their wooden fence, watching as they used their mother's gardening trowels to dig for treasure.

Mandy, unaware of Ruth's mother preparing lunch on the other side of the open window above them, had said, "My name's Mandy. My mom's got a big bush. Does yours?"

Ruth had thought about it for a moment, and then said, "Yes," at which point her mother barked Ruth's name in a tone Ruth had never heard before, and Mandy's face had disappeared from the fence.

Ruth hadn't seen much of Mandy in the years following that first interaction at the sandbox, but this afternoon Ruth and Sara had been walking home from school and were caught off guard when Mandy flung open the front door of the Cheswicks' house and yelled, "Ruth? *Hey, Ruth!*"

Ruth paused. She was, on the one hand, pleased to be noticed by Mandy, who was now in her first year at high school, but it was a peculiar sort of pleasure, one she didn't feel she ought to enjoy as much as she did.

"Hey, *Ruth!*" Mandy persisted.

"Yeah?" Ruth's voice faltered. She suddenly felt unsure of everything.

Mandy struck a pose in the doorway. Ruth recognized the pose from her father's magazines. Mandy's left leg, thrust out at an awkward angle, propped the screen door open, while her right hand reached up to clutch the doorjamb. The rest of Mandy's body strained to hold an impossibly contorted *S* shape.

Mandy wore white hot pants and a short, pink, terrycloth tube top, both of which were several sizes too small. Her breasts shimmied when she loosened her grip on the doorjamb to wave at Ruth. Puberty had been generous to Mandy, while it had not yet shown any interest in Ruth.

"Ruth, why don't you come on in here and have a drink with me?" Mandy hollered. "We ain't chatted in so long!"

Ruth was wary.

"We're supposed to go right home after school," she mumbled weakly, forcing her eyes away from Mandy's quivering curves and fixing her gaze instead on the line of moss that grew between the cracked slabs of the sidewalk.

"Silly, that doesn't mean you can't stop in for a quick *hello*." Mandy laughed but she sounded exasperated. "Come have a nice cold soda with me!"

Sara giggled shrilly behind her hand. Ruth had never heard anyone call it *soda* before. It was pop. Everyone knew that.

"Soda..." repeated Ruth, dubiously.

Mandy smiled and nodded. "Yeah! You know, it's hot out. C'mon in!"

"Well, okay..." Ruth said, making to walk up the driveway, but Sara pulled at her sleeve and whimpered. Ruth shook off Sara's hand and hissed, "Go on home if you're gonna be a baby." She took a deep breath and headed up the driveway, smiling tightly at Mandy's ample butt cheeks as she followed her into the house.

"So," Mandy was saying, "d'you ever babysit for the Parkers?"

Ruth sensed from Mandy's tone that babysitting for the Parkers was something she should want to do, even though the thought had never before crossed her mind. The Parkers, like the Cheswicks, had only boys who were not that much younger than Ruth. Babysitting them seemed unlikely. She shook her head.

"They're my favourite people to babysit for," Mandy said. "Mr. Parker is so nice, don't ya think?"

Mr. Parker had never struck Ruth as being particularly "nice." In fact, whenever Ruth saw Mr. Parker out front of his house, she crossed to the other side of the street and tried her best not to look at him. She felt he wanted to be looked at, which made her want to concentrate extra-hard on doing otherwise.

"Mr. Parker always treats me real nice," Mandy confided. She sat down at the table beside Ruth and flipped slowly through a dog-eared *Teen Beat* magazine. Mandy continued, "Too bad Mrs. Parker is such a bitch."

Their chat was interrupted then by a piercing wail from the side of the house where the Cheswick kids had been thumping. Mandy shot out of her chair and flew down the hall to the back door. Ruth heard the front door slam shut behind Sara. Ruth knew Sara was running home in a blind panic. She was afraid of the Cheswicks, and she was afraid of losing her TV privileges for being late after school.

Ruth heard Mandy bash open the aluminum screen door that led to the backyard and shout, "You shits better not try me today or I'll make you sorry, so help me *gawd*!" The screaming stopped abruptly, the back door slammed shut, and the thumping resumed. Mandy flounced back into the kitchen and slid into her chair with a sigh.

"Mr. Parker told me to call him Eddie," she went on. "Mrs. Parker is always riding his tail about one thing or another. She's *such* a nag. So poor Eddie likes how I stay after they get home from wherever they go and have a drink with him in the rec room so he can unwind. Has he ever made a drink for you?"

Mandy stared pointedly at Ruth. Ruth wished she had bolted with Sara when she'd had the chance.

"Eddie *always* likes to relax and have a drink with me in the rec room," Mandy continued. She adjusted her tube top. Her breasts jiggled a bit and then settled back down on top of her magazine. Corey Haim grinned up at Ruth from beneath a pink terrycloth nipple.

There was a faint buzz in Ruth's ears. She recognized this feeling. It felt like when she went swimming in the river near her grandmother's farm. Like when she strayed towards the deep water, where the willow tree fronds rippled slowly in the muddy current. The closer she got to the willows, the more the water temperature dropped, and the harder it was to keep her feet planted on the algae-slick rocks of the riverbed. She felt herself go absolutely still.

Mandy kept at it. "If you want, Ruth, you could, like, come with me next time. Eddie says I can bring my girlfriends over anytime I want." She paused and leaned closer to Ruth. Ruth could smell Cheez Whiz on Mandy's breath beneath the sweet stink of her Bonne Bell lip gloss and her Baby Soft perfume.

"I really like the time you and I spend together." Mandy's voice had grown syrupy, and she was staring intently at Ruth.

Ruth imagined the tips of her toes were now barely touching the riverbed. The murky water was lapping against her face and she had to crane her neck and tilt her chin up towards the sky to keep breathing.

"You and I are such good friends..." Mandy crooned.

Ruth squeezed her eyes shut, as if against the pointy rays of the sun, and water tickled into her ears, turning Mandy's voice to a low mumble.

"...aren't we, Ruth?"

Ruth gasped and jumped up from her chair, jarring the table and sloshing some of the pop out of her cup. "I can't swim here without my mom!" she blurted, bewildered and frantic.

"What?" Mandy wrinkled her nose and yanked her magazine away from the widening spill on the table.

Ruth snapped back into the present, surprised to find herself shivering in the Cheswicks' kitchen. "I gotta go!" Ruth shouted. She crossed her arms over her chest, clenched her fists under her armpits, and edged away from Mandy's cloying eyes and body, towards the hallway.

"All right, all right!" Mandy was yelling, a look of disgust pulling her pink lips into a sneer. "Jesus!"

Ruth ran to the front door and pounded on the handle till the latch gave.

"Hey!" hollered Mandy, leaning back in her chair to look down the hall as Ruth disappeared out the door. "Hey, whatever, *freak*!"

Ruth darted across the cool, shaded porch to the tarred black driveway that amplified the afternoon heat. She felt weak with relief, but also embarrassed. She heard the back door of the house crash open again, heard Mandy yelling at the boys to take off their goddamn shoes if they were coming inside.

Ruth paused on the sidewalk to catch her breath. She shielded her eyes from the glare of the sun with one hand, and squinted up at the Cheswicks' house, trying to make sense of what had just happened—or not happened—she wasn't sure. In the front window, the green curtains rippled slowly and then settled back against the screen, revealing nothing.

THE PRINCESS IS DEAD

THE SUN HAD BEGUN TO SET, but still his wife carried on. Andrews sulked in his backyard and poked at a clump of crabgrass with the toe of his slipper. He derived a perverse pleasure from his otherwise unblemished lawn. It had been touch and go for a few years in the late eighties. His wife and son had been lax in the training of the family dog, a corgi named Heather, but he had put an end to that by installing a patch of gravel at the side of the house, below the eaves, where the dog was confined twice daily by means of a short lead tied to a stake in the ground. Once the dog had thoroughly relieved herself on the gravel under Andrews' watchful eye, she was released and permitted the run of the yard without posing any risk to the lawn.

His next-door neighbour, Domingas, liked to watch the whole production over the fence with an amused look, and say, "You've got it all under control, don't you, boss?"

Andrews would give a curt nod, proud of his ingenuity, but not wanting to appear so.

Now, in the deepening suburban twilight, his lawn served as a salve for his nerves, which had been scraped raw by the wailing of his wife, Maureen. She sat glued to the television, watching the CBC's coverage of what appeared to be the sudden and—according to Maureen—globally devastating death of Princess Diana. A glance over his shoulder through the family room window reassured Andrews that he was better off in the yard, despite the growing darkness. Maureen was perched on the edge of the sofa, sodden tissue clutched in one hand and the phone in the other. She had called her best friend Rita, Domingas' wife, when Andrews had failed to be appropriately moved by the news. Her wet cheeks reflected the glow of the television screen. Maureen's lap cradled Heather, who looked indignant as the telephone cord swayed back and forth in front of her snout. Watching his wife of twenty years wail into the phone about the death of a woman she'd never met, Andrews was conscious of a stirring within him that signaled despair. And so, when Andrews heard the hum of the garage door opening, he beat a path across the lawn and through the side gate to be distracted by his son, who had returned from wherever it was that he went.

Out in front of the house, Andrews smiled absent-mindedly as Charles maneuvered the family's station wagon into the garage. Charles braked as the windshield was just shy of the tennis ball Andrews had suspended from the ceiling on a length of twine for Maureen.

"It's not my fault I can't see over the hood," she'd snapped when they'd learned the sensors on the automatic garage-door opener were not as sensitive to obstructions as they'd been led to believe.

Andrews had stood in the garage, surveying the damage and sucking on a toothpick, while he searched for an appropriate response to the situation. One side of the rear bumper hung from the station wagon by a bent piece of metal. The other side rested on the garage floor. They'd been unable to reverse the closing garage door once it had knocked off the bumper, so the door was now jammed at bumper level. Maureen claimed she had no way of knowing that she hadn't pulled the car all the way into the garage.

"My car," Andrews had finally said.

"Your car?" said Maureen. "That could have been my head! Think about that!"

Andrews thought about it.

"I've got to call Rita," Maureen had said, as she shuffled around the car and past Andrews to the door that led into the house. "She's not going to believe this. I could have been killed."

The door had slammed shut behind Maureen. A minute passed, and then the light on the automatic door opener had flicked off, leaving Andrews in the dark, his calves bathed in the orange glow of the street light out front.

Andrews pulled his gaze up from the repaired, but still dented, bumper and watched Charles slide out of the car and swing the door shut behind him in one fluid motion. There was no popping of joints, no groaning, no sign of exertion. Andrews felt proud, as though this physical ease was something Charles had learned from him, although he knew very well that wasn't the case. Andrews had never been fluid at anything.

Charles noticed his father standing behind the car.

"Hey," he said nonchalantly, and made for the door that led into the house.

"I wouldn't go in there if I were you," said Andrews.

Charles paused and turned to face his father with a bored expression.

"Your mother's in there having a bird over some car accident."

"You mean Princess Di?" Charles' face came to life. "Are they showing pictures of it yet?" He disappeared into the house.

"People die in car accidents every day!" Andrews called as the door slammed shut behind Charles. "Every day," he muttered to himself.

Andrews sighed and studied the street, knowing that any number of people could be watching him from behind their sheers. He knew this because when he wasn't tending to his lawn, he spent much of his time watching his neighbours from behind his own expanse of sheers. He enjoyed seeing each neighbour drive by in a car that revealed his or her shortcomings: rust marks, bald tires, filthy windows, crudely plagiarized handicap signs, dashboards obscured by outdated parking tickets. Rear windows crammed with bleached-out tissue boxes, stuffed animals, stained pillows, and abandoned action figures. None of it surprised Andrews, in light of the deplorable state of their lawns.

Of particular significance on his scale of poor car hygiene was Domingas, who had to park his dilapidated car in the driveway because his garage was filled with Rita's wholesale beauty-supply inventory. Domingas didn't seem to mind Rita's annexing of the garage. Rather, when Andrews had teased him about it, Domingas declared pride in his wife's entrepreneurship. This was driven home on Saturday mornings, when Andrews' station behind the sheers was more often than not blighted by a showy exchange between the couple after they'd loaded up the trunk of the car with reeking pink boxes. As Rita reversed down the driveway, she would flutter her fingers through the windshield at Domingas. Domingas would then kiss the fingers of his hand and flutter them back at Rita.

The only thing more disturbing to Andrews than this public display of affection was his fear that Maureen would one day catch sight of the Saturday Morning Domingas Ritual. Not only would she criticize him for the pleasure he derived from watching other people's private moments through the sheers, but, given her many complaints over the years about Andrews' lack of physical affection, Maureen might have grounds for a new complaint about how Andrews never fluttered his fingers at her.

The thought of fluttering his fingers at Maureen made Andrews shudder, and he surfaced out of his reverie to find that he was still standing in the driveway, clad only in his housecoat and slippers. He smacked his palm against the garage-door opener and returned to the privacy of his backyard.

Andrews eyed the wooden bench Maureen had forced him to place at a ridiculous angle against the back corner of their fence. He never sat there, because from that perspective, he was on display to all the rear bedroom windows of the houses on either side of his. He preferred instead to stick close to the deck that ran beneath his kitchen and living-room windows. But it was almost completely dark now, and the wooden bench looked more comfortable than the ornate wrought-iron furniture Maureen had purchased for the patio, so Andrews wandered over and sat down.

"I don't see what all the fuss is about."

The voice echoed his thoughts. Andrews jerked his head up and around to find Domingas glaring over the fence towards the light of Andrews' family room window.

"Domingas! You scared me."

"It's not like she'd have thought twice about that woman a day ago when she was still alive."

Andrews watched with incredulity as Domingas jutted his chin at Andrews' window.

"Ask me, that woman needs a hobby or something. Keep her mind engaged."

Although he was in complete agreement with Domingas, Andrews knew a line had been crossed. The obligation to defend Maureen's honour made him uneasy; he hated hypocrisy.

"Come again?" he said.

"Look at that," Domingas said. "You'd think she was a blood relative."

Andrews reluctantly swiveled around on the bench to peer through his living room window, and saw that Rita Domingas had joined Maureen on the couch. The pair dabbed at their eyes with tissues from a box positioned on the sofa between them. Heather must have been exiled to the floor. Charles's bedroom window upstairs glowed blue—he was watching the news alone in his room. Andrews realized that Domingas was criticizing Rita's grief, which meant he was not obliged to defend Maureen. His relief was so immediate he was afraid he'd whimpered out loud. He glanced back at Domingas. Domingas was scowling at the window.

"At least your wife's parents are British," Andrews said. He rummaged in the pocket of his housecoat for the bag of jujubes he had tucked away earlier.

"What's that got to do with it?"

"Maureen has no connection to England but you'd never know it from the way she's carrying on."

They fell silent, Domingas scraping the palm of his hand up and down the scruff on his cheek, Andrews chewing thoughtfully.

"Your lawn's looking fine, boss," said Domingas.

"There's some crabgrass over there by the air-conditioning compressor. I'll have to get at it in the morning before it spreads."

"Thing is, Rita hasn't let me touch her in six years."

Andrews choked on his jujube. He tried to be subtle as he retched into the palm of his hand.

Domingas continued. "We used to be at it all hours of the night and day when we were trying to have kids, but when we gave up on that, she gave up on everything."

A light went on in Andrews' kitchen window. He felt inexplicably saved. After a moment, they heard an electric whirring noise.

"Maureen," said Andrews. "She's into the frozen daiquiris."

"That wholesale gig was the best thing that ever happened to me. Rita leaves the house every Saturday morning and then I'm free until one. I've met someone, Andrews."

Andrews turned to stare slack-jawed at Domingas, the wet jujube still cupped in the palm of his hand. Out of the corner of his eye, he saw the kitchen light go off. He felt abandoned, adrift in the riptide of Domingas's admission.

"I wonder how long two people can go on living like this," Domingas said.

Andrews carefully put the jujube back into his mouth and wiped the palm of his hand on his housecoat.

"How old is your boy now, Andrews? Eighteen?"

"That's right," Andrews said, wary.

"I bet it never occurs to him that he could end up like this."

"Like what?"

Domingas scratched his whiskers and then sighed. "Never mind," he said. "Anyway, I'm leaving. Tonight. Rita doesn't know yet. Just thought I'd say goodbye."

"You're kidding," said Andrews, stunned.

"Take care, boss," said Domingas, and then he walked away.

"Sure. I mean, you too."

As he listened to his neighbour's footfalls fade, Andrews gazed up Charles's window. The erratic blue light of Charles' television jumped and pulsed. He was disappointed that it would not have occurred to Charles to join him in the yard. When Andrews was growing up, he'd admired his father, and valued his advice and attention. Andrews couldn't pinpoint when Charles had become so indifferent toward Andrews, but he was, and Andrews didn't know how to fix that. In the living room, Maureen sat back on the sofa, legs crossed. She sipped a daiquiri and cackled with Rita. The TV footage that had only minutes ago rendered her speechless with grief now went unnoticed. Such was the unpredictability of Maureen's emotional landscape. That unpredictability was a quality that had endeared her to him when they were first married, made him want to protect her, but it had long ago become exasperating. As he sat there contemplating the lackluster Saturday mornings of his near future, it slowly dawned on Andrews that the contrived and empty gestures of another man's dead marriage had been his only source of intimacy. He would miss the Saturday Morning Domingas Ritual like he missed every other illusion that had once sustained him: the meaningfulness of life, the institution of marriage, the value in stoicism, and the consolation of having had a son. Andrews realized that when Domingas had referenced the two people in an empty marriage, he'd been referring to them—to Domingas and Andrews.

Andrews removed his housecoat and folded it neatly on the bench beside him. Then, with some effort, he lowered himself, groaning and wincing, first onto his knees, and then his belly, so that he was lying face down in the cool, damp grass. It was prickly against his cheek, but he didn't mind. He ran his fingers back and forth though the springy turf, and inhaled its earthy scent. It was the scent of final destinations—something Andrews had not yet lost faith in. He closed his eyes and steeled himself as best he could, determined, as he was, to stay the course.

EMPTIES

Before

The watery light of dawn found Kerri, sixteen and, until recently, a student at Harmony Heights Secondary School, passed out on the picnic table. The long grass around the table was littered with empty beer bottles, cigarette butts, and an empty pizza box. Her best friend, Jolene, was curled up under a transparent plastic tarp on a foldable chaise lounge that was missing one arm.

When Kerri came to, she was shivering. Her feathered blonde hair was crushed flat on one side of her head and stuck to her damp face like a fringe of small wet tongues. Dean was sitting on the tabletop at her side, rubbing her denim-clad bum. Kerri grunted and sat up slowly. She slumped forward, her throbbing head cradled in her hands. Dean leaned over and murmured into her hair.

"F'goff," Kerri moaned, and elbowed him away. She put her head back in her hands and wondered if she'd pissed him off, but a wave of nausea quickly monopolized her attention. After a minute, she heard footsteps and looked up to see Dean stalking across the yard to the house, hand in hand with Jo, who looked like she'd won the lottery. Kerri watched them disappear through the screen door and then lay back down with a sigh.

When Kerri came to for the second time, the sun was peeking out from behind the house and she was sweating. The smell of cooking food wafting from the kitchen window coaxed her up off the picnic table and into the house.

Paula stood at the stove in a nightgown that had once been pink but had been washed into a gloomy shade that was somewhere between beige and grey. The fabric was pulled taut over her belly and her bare feet were cracked and grey with dirt. A cigarette dangled from her lips above a sputtering pan of ground beef. Kerri's stomach simultaneously turned and growled at the smell of food, smoke, and dirty dishes.

"Mornin'," she said to Paula. Paula said nothing. Kerri's hi-cuts stuck to the linoleum as she walked over to the kitchen sink. She ran the faucet until the water was cold and the sulphur smell had subsided, then pulled back her hair and leaned down into the crusty sink to drink from the tap.

Paula watched out of the corner of her eye for a minute. "My dad called."

"Huh?" said Kerri, straightening up and shutting off the tap.

"My dad called. He's comin' this afternoon. You know what *that* means."

"Mmm-hmm." Kerri nodded and wiped the smeared blue mascara off her face with the sleeve of her jean jacket.

"That means you's all gotta split or there's no way he'll give me any money."

Kerri slumped over the sink and salivated as she watched Paula break up the browning meat with the back of a bent metal spoon.

"Whatcha makin'?" asked Kerri.

"What's it *look* like I'm making?" barked Paula. She took the cigarette from her lips and leaned towards Kerri to flick her ashes into the sink. Kerri moved out of the way and then slumped back against the counter without taking her eyes from the pan.

Paula waited another minute and then yelled, "I'm makin' hamburger! What's it look like I'm makin'?" Under her breath, she said, "Moron." Paula and Kerri were the same age, but Paula acted like an old woman. They stood in silence until Kerri's stomach audibly growled.

"Smells good," said Kerri.

"Ya, well if you want some you better hurry up, cause my old man is comin' round and none of you's can be here when he does!" Paula smacked the spoon against the side of the pan and squeezed her left eye shut against the smoke of her cigarette. Kerri turned the tap back on to drink some more.

Paula yelled over the running water, "And tell them fuckers to clean up before you's all take off!"

During

That afternoon, Kerri and Jo laboured slowly down King Street towards the Beer Store. It was the first warm day of spring. Jo had the sleeves of her Leafs jersey pulled up over her shoulders and Kerri had tried to roll up the legs of her stretch jeans, but they only went up to the tops of her ankles before they got too tight. One side of her feathered hair was still matted flat against her skull, but she'd reapplied her blue mascara and her lips were coated in sticky pink gloss— the same as Jo's.

"This sucks," said Jo.

"Mm-hmm," said Kerri.

"We need one of them old-lady carts."

Their gait was halting and awkward. They each carried a six of empties in one hand, and in the other they had balanced between them two two-fours. It was more than they could handle, but Kerri had insisted the Beer Store wasn't too far of a walk. Kerri had never walked to the Beer Store before. The dimensions of downtown Oshawa, once so familiar as it whisked past her in the passenger seat of her dad's pickup, now seemed to stretch endlessly before her. By the time they'd reached King Street, nowhere near the halfway point, Kerri knew she'd made a mistake.

"Kerri, c'mon," Jo pleaded. "Let's just stick these in a bush or something and come back for them later."

"No way!" Kerri said. "Anyone could come and take them. And then what?"

Jo sighed, and they walked on in silence for a moment or two.

Jo sized up Kerri's eyelids, puffy and red behind their bright blue armour of makeup, and asked, "So what'd yer mom have to say when you called her?"

"Nothing much," mumbled Kerri. "Mostly she just cried and stuff."

"Think you can get her to admit your dad kicked you out?"

Kerri shrugged. The empties clinked.

"No way you'll get welfare if she doesn't," Jo said ominously, shaking her head.

"We're high school drop-outs, Jo," snapped Kerri. "Neither one of us is gettin' anything."

Jo sucked in the sides of her mouth and raised her eyebrow, but didn't say anything more.

They walked on. At one intersection they paused to pull the bottoms of their shirts up and out through their neck holes, creating makeshift bikini tops and exposing their hard, teenaged bellies to the downtown traffic. Jo had twisted her long dark hair up on top of her head and stabbed a twig through it to hold it in place. Occasionally, a passing car would honk.

"So," Jo continued, trying to mask the drudgery of their task with small talk, "how come Paula's dad doesn't live there with her?"

"He has a girlfriend," said Kerri. "He lives in her trailer with her."

"And he just comes around on welfare day to give Paula money?" asked Jo, incredulous.

"Yup."

"She's fuckin' lucky."

"No kidding, eh?"

"Does Paula know her mom?"

"Yeah, she grew up with her mom, but her mom's crazy. When Paula told her she was pregnant, her mom told her to get rid of it, and then she, like, gave her a black eye, so Paula left."

"Huh," said Jo, mulling it all over. "Doesn't her dad hit her?"

"Sometimes, but I guess it isn't so bad since he's never around. Besides, now that she's preggers, he won't lay a hand on her."

The girls stopped and put down their beer cases. They walked round the front of the cases to switch sides. They paused, squinting at the sun and kicking at the dirt until their fingers stopped screaming.

Jo said, "I'm fuckin' dyin' for a smoke."

Kerri bent down, slid the edges of the beer case handles into the deep grooves on her fingers, and said, "You ready?"

Jo nodded, and they picked up the cases and resumed their slow, lopsided gait.

"So how'd you meet Paula, anyway?" asked Jo.

"Home Ec," said Kerri.

The girls were taking a break in the shade of a rusted billboard frame. Behind them, the broken concrete of an empty parking lot gave way to anemic crabgrass and dirt. At the far end of the lot, the brick wall of a defunct car wash read, "We'll Make You Shine."

They sat on their beer cases, flipping the bird at any cars that honked.

Kerri found a dry, yellowed cigarette butt in the gutter beside them. It still had a couple hauls' worth of tobacco in it, so she ripped off the filter, stuck the torn end in her mouth, and held Dean's Zippo against the burnt end. Jo's eyebrows twitched when she saw the lighter, but she said nothing. Kerri snapped the Zippo shut with a flick of her wrist and handed it to Jo, who tucked it into her pocket and let her hand linger briefly over its shape beneath her jeans.

Kerri puffed gingerly, squinting as bits of loose tobacco caught light and flew up in the breeze. She said, "This one day in class? Ms. Bayner was holding up these kitchen utensils, okay? And she was all, 'What's this one was for?'" Kerri paused to hold the cigarette out to Jo, and with her other hand pulled a strand of tobacco from her tongue.

"She held up this thing we'd bought my mom for Christmas. Each year we fill her stocking with, like, kitchen stuff, even though it makes her mad. My dad's just like, whatever."

"Prick," said Jo.

"So anyway, I was like, 'That's a potato masher!' and Ms. Bayner like, laughs, and then *every*one laughs. Ms. Bayner was all, 'Well, that's very creative, Kerri, but what's it *really* for?' and everyone else was, you know, giggling and shit."

"Bitches," Jo said.

"Totally." Kerri nodded. "But Paula never laughed. She just sat there and, like, looked at me, or whatever. We started hanging out after that. I felt bad for thinking she was trash at first. She's not so bad once you know her."

"Sure," said Jo, though she didn't sound convinced.

They sat for a while longer, and then Jo asked, "So what *was* that thing, anyway?"

Kerri rolled her eyes. "I can't remember what it's called. But it's, like, this metal circle with a plastic handle on one part of it, and slits on the other. For making pastry or whatever."

"Oh."

"Yeah. As if I'll ever be making pastry for some fat fuck. Why am I gettin' graded on this?"

Jo laughed. "Ladyfriend, if that ever happens, you call me pronto, 'cause that is something I'd pay money to see."

Kerri smirked and spat in the gutter.

It took them another hour of walking to reach the Beer Store. Jo spent the last half hour near tears, but Kerri ignored her and kept her eyes locked on the friendly orange sign that hovered like a second sun above the distant rooftops. Once they'd heaved their cases up onto the metal conveyor belt, Kerri went outside and sat on the yellow curbstone in the parking lot. Jo stayed inside with the empties, sighing theatrically while she waited for the beer guys to stop ignoring her.

Kerri hummed to herself and smiled up into the sun. Her fingers were still throbbing and she couldn't raise her arms without considerable effort, but they'd made it, and now they were going to have some money. Money for food and smokes and the bus. Money they had earned, and could spend on whatever they damn well pleased.

It felt good thinking about what she might like to do. She could smell the lake on the breeze, and she thought maybe later, when they were done scavenging for more bottles, she and Jo could get down to the waterfront and still be back before sundown. Maybe even have an ice cream while they were at it. Kerri hadn't dared to think this way when she was living at home because her days at home had all been the same. Tightness in her chest and throat. Sitting still in her bedroom with the door closed, tracking her dad's every movement in the house. What room was he in? Had he just sighed? Was he mad? Was he coming?

But she didn't live there anymore, and better yet, her dad didn't know where she was. She was free. Sitting there in the sunny Beer Store parking lot, faced with the unknown possibilities of an afternoon that was hers to fill as she pleased, Kerri felt a surge of something big and bright and endless fill her up till she thought she might burst wide open right there on the concrete. She closed her eyes and took a deep breath, surprised to feel herself on the verge of tears.

"Goddamn!" hollered Jo as she sailed out through the sliding glass doors, trying unsuccessfully to raise her trembling arms above her head in triumph. "We got six fuckin' dollars!"

"No way," laughed Kerri. She turned her face away from Jo, blinked back her tears, and swallowed hard. "Didn't he check for BT holes?"

"Obviously not." Jo extended her hand down to Kerri. "Today is our lucky day." She pulled Kerri up to her feet.

"No kidding," said Kerri. She brushed the dust from her bum.

Jo was snapping her fingers and skipping towards the sidewalk. "So now what, ladyfriend?" she called over her shoulder.

"Well," said Kerri, holding her lower back and pushing her belly out front of her in a stretch, "I think we should do like Paula said and check people's yards and shit for more empties."

"Fuck that," said Jo. "Let's get smokes."

"Who's gonna buy them for us?"

Jo pulled the twig out of her hair and struck a pose. "Bitch, who *wouldn't* buy them for us?"

Buying cigarettes downtown turned out to be hard. At school, there was always a senior who would buy you a pack if you let them keep a few cigarettes from your pack as a fee. But downtown in the middle of the day, the adults turned stone-faced as soon as Jo or Kerri approached them. After an hour or so of wandering they finally got lucky with a sad-eyed woman who said she used to be just like them. Kerri and Jo had laughed about that as they headed for Kinsmen Park.

"As if," said Jo. "Did you see that hag? She was never like us."

"Her nic stains were practically brown," said Kerri, looking nervously at the first two fingers of her right hand.

"You can rub lemon on them. Your fingers. My mom read it in her *Chatelaine*."

Kerri looked up at Jo. "You think that'll save us?"

"From what? Being a fuckin' Debbie Downer? No, that's totally your future. But at least your fingers won't look like hers."

Kinsmen Park was part of a green valley that cut through the whole city, top to bottom, with a creek in the middle that ran through culverts and under bridges until it emptied into Lake Ontario. Kerri used to crane her neck to catch a glimpse of it on the bus ride to her high school.

"Hey, let's go down to the creek," said Kerri. "There's probably a few empties down there—we can get some more coin."

"No way," said Jo. "See that tree?" She pointed up at the crest of the eastern side of the valley, where a line of trees marked the edge of the park. "That tree has our name on it.

Last one there gets a punch in the arm."

Kerri laughed as she watched Jo run the first few feet up the hill and then pretend to have a heart attack.

"Who's the Debbie Downer now?" shouted Kerri as she sprinted past Jo's corpse. Kerri didn't look back, but she could hear Jo laughing and swearing behind her as they pseudo-raced up the hill.

When they reached the top, gasping and coughing and spitting, they sprawled out on their backs beneath a maple tree. Jo lit two Dunhills and passed one to Kerri. "You juiced it," Kerri said, wrinkling her nose at the soggy filter.

"Ahhhh, it doesn't get any better than this," sighed Jo, ignoring her.

"No shit," agreed Kerri, her face turned up to watch the leaves above her flit from green to silver and back again in the sun. "This is livin'."

"Miller time," aped Jo, and Kerri snickered.

They smoked in contented silence and watched a man down in the park playing fetch with his orange dog.

"Think you'll go back to school one day?" asked Jo.

Kerri pulled thoughtfully at her smoke and exhaled with a sigh. She didn't really give a shit, but she knew Jo was worried about it. Jo's older brother had said they were making a big mistake by dropping out like he had done. Now he stole cars for people who wanted to scam their insurance.

"Probably," Kerri said eventually. "Maybe when I'm older and I got nothin' better to do. While I'm young I just want to, like, live. You know?" She looked over at Jo. Jo was nodding.

The dog had climbed partway up the hill toward them and was walking in tight, frantic circles. The man put his hands in his pockets and waited.

Jo said, "This is so awesome. Dean and those guys are idiots, eh? They totally shoulda just come with us instead of fucking around at the arcade." Kerri didn't really mind their absence, but agreed anyway.

Jo said, "Dean and I are totally gonna get married. I can just tell. Can't you just tell?" She looked brightly at Kerri. When Jo's parents had divorced, her mom had drawn the blinds in the living room and collapsed on the couch with a migraine. She'd been there every day since, and that was three years ago. Kerri had met Jo's mom. Her face was just as washed out as Paula's crummy old nightgown.

"Married," said Jo, watching as the dog finished up its business and then galloped in a long, wide arc towards its master. "You think he's gonna stay out of jail long enough to get married?"

"Totally," said Jo. "He's got my brother to show him how it's done. They're gonna make a killing. Hey," Jo said, hitting Kerri's leg with the back of her hand. "What about you? Think you'll get hitched one day?"

Kerri thought about her parents. They'd stayed together for reasons that were beyond Kerri, as they obviously hated each other. She suspected their miserable marriage persisted *because* of her.

"Doubt it," said Kerri.

"Really? Not even if you're in love with someone?"

Kerri chewed on her lip and scowled at the grass, deep in thought. "Nah," she finally said.

Jo looked at her with disbelief and then looked away. "Huh," she said, under her breath.

Kerri frowned. "Well, I don't know…Fuck," she said.

"Being in love is the shit, Kerri. You'll understand more when it happens to you."

"Well, you didn't ask me about love, did you, Jo? You asked if I was gonna get married. They got nothin' to do with each other."

Jo was suddenly furious. "Marriage *is* love, Kerri! You just think that way because of your parents! You shouldn't let them fuck it all up for you like that."

"Well, tell me, Jo. Didn't your parents love each other when they swore in front of God and everyone that they'd stay together no matter what?"

"Shut up."

"Wasn't that love, Jo? D'you think they knew they were gonna wind up all pissed off and divorced when they were in *love*?"

"Fuck you!" yelled Jo, with enough force to echo off the field below. The man and the dog both looked up at them.

Kerri lowered her head and focused on digging a little hole in the dirt beside her with her fingernail.

After a while, Jo muttered, looking straight ahead, "This is different. Me and Dean."

After

The streetlights were flickering as Kerri and Jo walked arm in arm up the street towards Paula's. They were singing, "Tangerine, Tangerine..." in melodramatic nasal voices. When they turned up the walkway, Kerri stopped singing but Jo continued, "Living reflect-shu-huns, from a dream..." Kerri shushed her and punched her on the arm.

"Hey! What's yer damage all of the sudden?" whined Jo, rubbing her shoulder.

"I dunno," said Kerri, who'd stopped halfway up the walk and was staring up at the house. "Just, what if he's still in there?" She jutted her chin up at the darkened windows and tried to cram her hands into her pockets. They wouldn't go, because her jeans were too tight, so she crossed her arms in front of her instead.

"Who?" asked Jo.

"Paula's dad." Kerri and Paula both acted tough in their own way, but both knew what it was like to feel terrorized and helpless. Jo didn't know; she just had an older brother who adored her.

"Well then," Jo said. "We'll just ask ol' Daddy Warbucks for some of his fine cash moneys! Besides," she continued, bouncing up the porch steps while Kerri hung back, "we're just a couple of Paula's friends dropping by to see if she wants to hang out. Right?"

Without waiting for Kerri's response, Jo rapped brusquely on the front door. The girls waited. Jo knocked again, and Paula swung open the door and stared stonily at her.

Jo put on a snooty accent and said, "Would the *man* of the house be in?"

Paula said, "You're looking at her." She turned on her heel and walked away. Jo sashayed into the hallway, opened the door wider, and bowed deeply towards Kerri.

"Madam," she said.

Kerri walked silently past Jo.

Jo straightened up and said, "You're welcome!" She swung the door shut and followed Kerri down the hall.

In the kitchen, the bare bulb that hung from the ceiling gave off a dull orange glow through its patina of grease. The air was blue and wispy with cigarette smoke and smelled faintly of bacon. Paula sat at the table, still wearing her nightgown, smoking a cigarette and jimmying one leg up and down. She balanced a coffee mug of RC Cola on her large belly, which had begun to round and harden.

Kerri and Jo stood. There was only one chair. Jo was telling Paula about their day.

"I'll tell you one thing, though," Jo was saying. "That was the hardest six bucks I ever earned. Nearly tore my fucking arm out of its socket." She gingerly rotated one arm in a circle and winced.

"More like the *only* six bucks you ever earned," said Paula, as she ashed her smoke in an empty potato chip bag. "D'you's get any other empties like I said to?"

Kerri glared at Jo.

Jo said, "Time got away from us today, but we'll be back out there first thing in the morning."

Paula rolled her eyes.

"What about you, Paula," asked Kerri. "How's yer dad?"

"Well, that's the thing—" But she was interrupted by an excited "Goddamn!" from Jo, who had opened the fridge.

"Look at all the grub in here!" Jo hollered. Paula bolted up from her chair, positioned her body between Jo and the fridge, and slammed the fridge shut with her hip. Jo backed up with her hands in the air and said, "Whoa!"

Paula pointed her finger in Jo's face and seethed, "My dad's on to you. He says you all gotta stay away!"

"Whaddaya mean he's *on* to us?" Jo demanded, lowering her hands to her hips. Kerri shook her head and chewed the inside of her cheek.

"He saw the state of this place," Paula yelled. "He knew I been havin' people round!"

"Well, you didn't tell him we were *staying* here, did ya?"

"No, but he knew—"

"Oh, bullshit, Paula!" Jo cut her off. "How'd he know unless you *told*?"

"*Listen*!" hollered Paula. "It's *my* fuckin' house and I'm tellin' ya my dad wants all yer asses outta here and that's *final*!"

She turned to grab her smokes from the table and muttered, "Or else he's callin' the cops."

Jo looked at Kerri. Kerri looked at the floor. Jo shook her head and walked over to the screen door that lead to the backyard. She pressed her forehead against the screen and said, "Great."

Through the screen they could hear crickets and someone's mom calling them in for the night. The trees and the rooftops were black silhouettes against the darkening sky. From the living room, they heard the metallic twang of the TV turning on, then the sound of canned applause floated down the hallway followed by, "Wheel–of–*Fortune*!"

The three girls were sitting in the dark living room, their faces pinched in the TV's flickering blue light, when they heard a car door slam out front. Kerri and Paula started and glanced towards the window, but the nicotine-stained curtains were drawn. Jo jumped up and disappeared down the hall. They heard her open the front door and yell, "Hey, baby!" and then a bunch of guys were talking and laughing and filling the hall with heavy footfalls and the clink of beer bottles. Kerri glanced at Paula, but Paula was glaring at the TV.

"Look what the cat dragged in!" Jo came around the corner with Dean in tow. He was followed by Jo's brother, Chris, and his friend Jerry, who were each carrying a case of beer.

"Why you sittin' in the dark?" said Jerry, as he smacked on the overhead lights. Only one of the light fixtures worked, and it was over by the dining table. A gaunt man with wiry red hair and a sallow complexion lingered by the door. Kerri hadn't seen him before. He looked old. The other guys were all around nineteen, but the new guy looked like he could have been in his thirties.

Dean extracted himself from Jo's embrace.

"This here," said Dean, putting his arm around the man's bony shoulders and jerking him side to side, "this here's my good buddy Paul. A friend of the family."

Kerri smiled at him. Jo said, "Howdy, Paul!"

Paula didn't say anything, and neither did Paul.

"Paul just got in from Vancouver this morning, so we thought we should celebrate. I haven't seen Paul in years, ain't that the truth, Paul?" said Dean.

Paul said, "Yup."

"Hitchhiked all the way," said Chris.

"No *way*," said Kerri, in awe. Paul smiled and nodded.

In a goofy voice, Dean said, "*Paul*-a, meet Paul! Paul, this is *Paul*-a!" Jo giggled but Paula kept staring at the TV, scrutinizing the *Wheel of Fortune* credits that were flying up the screen. Jo and Dean exchanged a look.

Dean staggered over to the couch and sat down beside Paula. Her arms were crossed and she raised her shoulders up around her ears when Dean tried to rub them. "Paula. Wassa matter, darlin'?" asked Dean in a syrupy voice.

"Fuck off," she said. But her edges were clearly softening, so he kept it up.

"Paula, tell Dean wassa matter. Don't you wanna drink the nice beer I bought special for you?" He held out his hand. Chris pulled a bottle from his case and smacked it into Dean's waiting palm. Everyone was smiling now except for Jo, who stood in the doorway beside Paul, glowering at Dean.

Dean kept his eyes on Paula, cracked the cap off the beer, put his arm around her shoulders, and held the bottle up to her grinning lips. His mouth was almost touching her ear. "Paula," murmured Dean. "Why don't you have a nice cold beer and tell Dean all about your daddy's visit."

Jo piped up from the doorway. "She said he's calling the cops on us."

"*What*?" Dean slammed the beer on the coffee table and stood up. He stared at Paula like he was about to hit her. Paula shied away from him. Dean was on parole. He'd only been out of jail for a month. Theft Under, and assault.

It was Paula's turn to try and smooth things over. She grabbed the foaming beer from the table, shook her head, and said, "No, no, no, it ain't like that at all!" She took a sip of foam.

"Why don't you tell us how it is, then?" said Jo.

"Well, you shouldn't go twisting my words like that, *Jo*!" Paula snapped. Paul had backed all the way up into the hallway and was trying to catch Jerry's eye.

"Listen," Paula said. She held up her hands and kept smiling at Dean. "I can handle my old man. All's I'm tryna say is that you's should help out more around the house. I ain't yer fuckin' maid."

Kerri looked at the guys. Chris was the only one who'd made an attempt to help Kerri and Jo clean earlier. The rest of them had taken off as soon as Kerri had yelled up the stairs through a mouth full of ground beef that Paula's dad was coming? None of them looked chastened now.

Dean looked at Jo with disbelief. "Jo, didn't I tell you to help Paula clean this morning? She can't do it all on her own!" Paula raised her head and closed her eyes, savouring the victory.

"*Dean*!" Jo stamped her foot and opened her mouth to let loose, but Jerry cut in.

"Look, man, if there is any chance at all of pigs I'm fucking outta here." He chugged his beer, slammed the empty back in his case, and began pulling his coat back on. Jerry was the only one in the group with a job and a car and money. His co-op placement had hired him the summer after grade eleven, and he'd never gone back to school. He cleaned air ducts for a living and had a company van. They all relied on him.

Paul's voice floated in from the hallway. "I don't need no heat, man. Fuck this."

Dean sighed. "All right, that's *it*!" Paula flinched. Dean flipped his long hair back over each shoulder and pulled back the bandana he wore over his head.

Paula tried to melt into the corner of the couch.

"Can everybody just chill the fuck out for a second?" Dean stormed over to the doorway. "Paul!" he yelled. "Get the fuck back in here and sit down!" They all heard the front door shut, and Paul reluctantly reappeared. Dean spun around to face Paula. The tassels on his leather jacket slapped against his back.

"Paula, is yer dad callin' the cops or isn't he?"

Paula was on the verge of tears. "No."

"You're absolutely fucking sure?"

"*Yes*!"

"All right!" said Dean. "So can everyone just relax?"

Chris caught Kerri's eye. He rolled his eyes and then winked at her. She lowered her head and smiled at her hi-cuts.

Dean sighed and flopped back down on the couch next to Paula. He shook his head slowly and looked at the TV. "Fucking *Jeopardy!*," he said. Chris handed him a beer. Dean gestured to Jo and she scrambled over to the couch to curl up beside him. Paul sat down near the hallway where he could keep an eye on the front door, and Jerry opened a beer for him.

Dean elbowed Paula and said, "Check out *this* fucking goof, eh?" He pointed at a *Jeopardy!* contestant who was licking his lips and rubbing the side of his nose. Paula laughed her loud laugh, and the conversation began to flow. Kerri told Jerry about the dog she'd seen in the park. It had reminded her of his.

Paul said, "What is Uzbekistan?" The *Jeopardy!* contestant echoed him and won the lightning round. Dean laughed, shook his head, and said, "You edumacated fuck." Paul grinned and held up his beer for cheers.

As the evening wore on, the conversation deteriorated into the usual drunken shouting match. According to Dean, the real problem with people today was that no one had any respect. The guys all agreed with him on this point, and there was a moment of quiet, until Jerry broke the silence with an underhanded remark about the Leafs, and then everyone started shouting again.

Paula had fallen asleep in front of the TV, despite all the noise. Kerri was lying on the floor smoking a cigarette and staring off into space. Jo stood up and said she was going for a walk. Kerri got up and followed her out into the backyard.

They wandered over to the picnic table and sat down.

"Too bad we don't have a tent," said Kerri. "I'd totally sleep out here again."

"Yeah," said Jo, wistfully. "Those shit-for-brains'll be shoutin' all night about who can take who, and blah fuckin' blah."

Kerri laughed.

"Swear to God," Jo continued. "They think they're such hot shit." She stood up and began sweeping her right foot through the long grass, looking for something.

Kerri said, "Yeah. When's the last time me and you sat around talkin' about how we're better than everybody else?"

"Exactly. Fucking blowhards."

Kerri heard a metallic clink in the grass under Jo's foot. Jo heard it too, and bent down to pick up a beer cap. She put it in her pocket and continued her search.

Jo said, "So, like, seriously though, Chris is pissed at me for dropping out."

"Sounds about right," said Kerri. "Big brother and all."

"Oh, as if!" Jo rolled her eyes. "He's a drop-out too, in case you hadn't noticed."

"I know, I know, I'm just saying. Big brother. He's just, like, looking out for you or whatever."

"You think it was stupid to drop out?" Jo asked.

Kerri shrugged. "So they say."

"But you don't think so?" Jo watched Kerri, her head tilted to one side.

Kerri leaned back and looked up at the sky. There were no stars. Just a dull, dark pink dome of trapped light from the car plant down the street. She said, "I don't know. I just kinda wanna figure it out for myself." She looked over at Jo. Jo stood there, waiting. Kerri frowned. "Its just like, people don't really know what the fuck they're talking about. They just repeat the same old crap. Like what's been told to them. You know?" She waited for Jo to nod in agreement, but Jo only tilted her head.

"So I'm like, what if everyone is full of shit? What if it's all downhill from here? Because seriously, Jo, if I get all old and sad and shit? And I find out then, when it's too late that, like, everyone was blowin' smoke up my ass about what *really* matters? Like with school and parents and whatever? And I wasted all my fucking life tiptoeing around and being scared to breathe and doing whatever I'm told to do? I swear, I'll fucking *lose* it." She kept her voice strong, but quiet. "I swear to God I will." She looked at Jo.

Jo stared back at her.

"Seriously!" Kerri was agitated. "Think about it!"

Jo looked down and fiddled with the beer caps in her pocket.

Kerri sighed. "I don't know," she said. "I'm young. I'll fix things if I'm wrong. But I don't think I am."

Jo walked back to the picnic table and dumped a pile of bottle caps on the table beside Kerri.

"You sound like a lunatic," she said.

Kerri let out a long, strained sigh. "You should totally be a therapist. You'd be really good at it. Real helpful, like."

Jo picked one of her caps and turned to face the yard. At the back of the lot, a build-it-yourself shed had been abandoned halfway through the build-it-yourself process. It leaned dejectedly against the fence. Lying face down in the grass between Jo and the shed were the flattened shards of a broken Mr. Turtle pool. The sun had bleached them out to the colour of pistachio ice cream. In the dark, partially hidden in the overgrown lawn, they resembled the picked-clean rib cage of a large animal.

"One drink for the pool, two for the shed," said Jo. She held her hand up beside her ear, pointed her elbow at the shed, and snapped a beer cap from between her thumb and middle finger. It disappeared without a sound into the grass beside the pool.

"Looks like you'll be sober in no time," said Kerri, as she stood up and grabbed a handful of caps. She snapped one and it sailed into the neighbour's yard.

Jo threw her head back and crowed, "That's what you get, smartass!"

Kerri grinned and readied her next shot.

They stood there for a while, pinging the occasional cap off of the shed or the pool, hollering when they got a hit, swearing under their breath when they missed. They were both laughing hysterically at nothing in particular when the perpetually shirtless man who lived next door shouted over the fence at them to shut up. Kerri looked back over her shoulder at the house to see if Dean had heard, while Jo bent double, gasping and giggling helplessly into her hands.

Kerri shushed her, not wanting to provoke the neighbour. They'd only been staying with Paula for a few days but they already knew the guy was a yeller.

"Maybe we should go inside," Jo said when she'd caught her breath. "We're outta caps anyway."

"You go. I'm gonna hang out here for a while."

"And do what?"

"I don't know." Kerri shrugged.

Jo paused, her feet in the long yellow rectangle of light from the screen door that stretched out across the grass, and watched Kerri lie down on her back on the picnic table.

"You're not seriously gonna sleep out here again?" asked Jo. She glanced at the clear plastic tarp, still strewn across the broken chaise lounge, and hugged herself. "Last night sucked."

"I dunno," said Kerri. Her voice was flat. "Maybe."

Jo eyed Kerri with suspicion. "What's the matter?"

"Nothing."

"Come inside."

"I said no!" Kerri snapped.

"Well, what's your fucking problem?"

"Nothing!" Kerri shouted. She didn't know why she was shouting. She glanced over and saw that Jo looked hurt.

Kerri sighed and said, "Nothing. I'm just bored, is all." She was embarrassed at how her voice trembled when she spoke, even though she had no intention of crying. She turned her face away from Jo. Jo hesitated for a moment longer, and then walked quietly into the house.

Kerri listened to the sounds coming from inside. Jo was talking and laughing with the guys. The reggae theme from *COPS* was playing on the TV, and Paula was awake and singing along half-heartedly in her low, off-key voice. In the next yard over, the hiss of the neighbour's hose was steady as he watered his lawn. The more Kerri was aware of all that went on outside her, without her, the smaller she felt. She stretched out her arms, gripped the edges of the table, and tried to focus on the rise and fall of her chest.

Hours had passed, and all the other sounds from the house and everywhere else were quiet, when Dean appeared at the side of the picnic table. He didn't say anything. Kerri knew that Jo was probably sleeping on the couch inside, and that Dean was bored, and that he would try to take Kerri's hand and lead her up the back staircase to one of the spare bedrooms like he'd done before. Kerri remembered how she'd felt in the Beer Store parking lot when she'd thought the whole day was hers. She'd felt full and strong. The opposite of how she felt when she was at home with her parents. The opposite of how she felt now. Kerri stood up and walked over to the broken chaise lounge. She scrunched up the tarp that Jo had slept under.

"What're you doing with that thing?" asked Dean.

"Nothing," said Kerri, as she tucked the tarp under her arm. She headed towards the street.

"Where are you going?"

"Nowhere."

Kerri knew that sounded like no answer, but she'd come to realize that nothing and nowhere was better than here and now. She'd make the rest up with time.

LOUIS REMEMBERS

"OKAY, FOLKS!" said Marge. "Now it's time to put all those skills you've learned to *work*!" She clapped her hands together. "I'm going to count you off into groups of four and we're going to do some *role* playing!"

We watched Marge gesture toward each audience member as she counted to eight, over and over again, until she had designated numbers to all of us. Those of us at the back watched her closely, trying to count ahead to discern our group members. Would we end up with losers? I was a five. Someone across the room gave me a "Now we're friends!" smile.

"Now, before you all head off into your new groups, let me tell you how we're going to do this," Marge said. "Two of you will be the disputants. You will argue. Of course, it's a *pretend* argument..." she paused here, so we could laugh. No one did. "And the other two will decide who will be the mediator and who will be the observer. The mediator will try to move the couple's argument *through* the triggers and into *processing*, using the techniques we've been learning over the past few weeks. Remember—no value judgments here, and use your active listening skills. The observer and the disputants will give the mediator constructive feedback at the end of the exercise. Does anyone have any questions?" The room was silent. "Alright, folks, let's *process*!" She clapped her hands again. I think we were supposed to be invigorated by her clapping, but for a moment no one moved, and then all at once there was the murmuring of numbers and the scraping of chairs across linoleum.

I was at the Learning Circle to attend this dispute resolution course with my friend Angela. She thought she could save her doomed relationship by springing the patented "Processing Pain, Garnishing Gain" techniques we were learning on her surly, unemployed boyfriend. He had refused to participate in anything offered through the Learning Circle, claiming it was a magnet for needy people with too much money. After a couple of classes, I could see he wasn't far off the mark, but Angela had begged me to come with her, no doubt so we could be united in self-righteousness when her partner failed to respond to the "powerful, proven techniques to release the healing power of mutual respect and understanding." She had offered to pay my course fee, and she knew I had nothing better to do on Thursday nights—or any other night, really. So here I was, learning how to facilitate meaningful communication with a room full of enablers.

The woman I'd caught smiling, Susan, had made a beeline for me at the clapping of Marge's hands. "I'm Susan," she said, touching the corner of her name tag with her fingertips, "and you look like a friend."

"I'm a five," I said.

"Oh, look!" she chirped, fluttering her fingers towards the front of the room.

I turned and saw a young woman, about my age, standing awkwardly beside a middle-aged man. The man was immaculately dressed and sweating profusely. He grinned and waved us over to them. Fives.

"Alright," I said to Susan. "Let's get busy."

"Hee hee!" giggled Susan.

We introduced ourselves, even though we were wearing name tags. Louis was there with his wife, and he pointed her out to us with pride. She held a notebook and a pen. She saw him pointing and gave us a cheerful wave. We all waved back. Anne was also there with her partner, a shy-looking man who blushed and shrugged when he saw us looking at him. Susan was one of the few people who was there without a significant other. No surprise there, I thought. I was also single, which I imagined didn't strike any of them as a surprise, either.

As we finished our introductions, Marge came around and asked us if we'd decided who were going to play the disputants. "We're going to repeat this exercise *four times*, so everyone will get a chance to try *each role*," she reassured us, as though we were all dying to pretend to be angry with a total stranger.

"I'll get it over with," I said. "Who's gonna be my victim?" I looked at Susan and Anne.

"I will!" said Louis. Susan and Anne exchanged looks while Louis scraped his chair noisily over to my side.

"Great work, folks!" said Marge. She jovially slapped Louis on the back and moved on to the sixes.

Susan and Anne made a big production about who would be mediator and who would be observer.

"Whatever you want, dear. It doesn't matter to me."

"No, no, no, please, you pick. I don't want to pick."

And so on.

Marge was clapping her hands again. "People! People!" The din died down a bit. "Remember to keep the arguments impersonal. We don't want you to get too deep into character. Make something up that you don't feel too attached to, about an issue that's not going to upset either of you, and remember—you're only *acting*."

We all nodded. There was some waggling of fingers and raucous laughter from the twos. I turned towards Louis. I was trying to think of mundane topics that people fought about. Louis turned to me and said, "Lynn, I'd like to suggest a topic, if it's alright with you."

"Sure, man," I said. "Go for it."

Louis smiled and pulled thoughtfully at a bit of lint on his pant leg. I smiled back.

"I'd like to talk about something I've seen that stays very present in my mind."

"Okay," I said, happy to oblige, wondering if this was now Louis in character or Louis preparing for his character. I settled back in my chair.

"Lynn," he began in a conversational tone, "when I was a young boy, I saw something. And, as I said, it stays very present in my mind." He rested his clasped hands in his lap and tilted his head, his eyes distant. He smiled as though he were recalling a fond memory. This didn't seem like much of a tiff, I thought, but what the hell. Susan and Anne were leaning forward, curious.

"We had many workers in my hometown," he continued. "Men who worked in the mine all day. It was very hard work, as I'm sure you can imagine." He winked. I couldn't really imagine, having always lived in a city of three million. My hard work was limited to clearing the occasional table while the busboy was out back for a smoke. I smiled and nodded, but I wondered if he might be having a go at me.

"One day, when I was just a small boy, I was playing in the dirt lane behind the houses when one of those men came home from his day's labour. The man walked into his house to find his wife with another man."

I felt myself stiffen. Susan and Anne's eyes grew very large. One of them, probably Susan, said, "Oh my."

I searched Louis' face for some indication of where he was going with this story. His hands were still resting in his lap. His head was still tilted, and his face was relaxed. He was gazing off into the distance with such dreamy affection that I chided myself for taking it so seriously.

Louis shook his head slowly, still smiling, and continued. "And so the man dragged his wife into laneway by her hair. She was naked. And her children were there with her. They were little and they were screaming."

"Uh...Louis..." I said.

He ignored me. "And the woman was screaming. And the husband knelt on one knee, in the dirt, pulling his struggling wife down with him. We all, my friends and I, stood there and watched. We knew the woman had shamed him—"

"Louis," I interjected, my voice wavering. My hands were sweating. "I don't want to talk about this—"

"And it was understood—" he raised his voice slightly to talk over my nervous protest "—that she must pay for that. So we stood and watched as he raised her head up by her hair, and then he brought it down with all his force, smashing her nose and shattering her teeth against the earth..."

"Louis, *seriously*!"

My eyes scanned the room for Marge. She was hunched over the eights, talking in a low voice. Angela was enjoying her sixes, bent double at the waist, laughing and slapping her thigh. Louis' voice had risen again. On the other side of the room, Louis' wife was nodding encouragingly to one of the fours.

Susan and Anne were shrinking into their chairs.

"...and he lifted her head up and she was bleeding so much, and crying, and then he smashed her face down again into the earth."

"Okay, stop," I said forcefully, holding my hands up at him. A couple of the eights raised their eyebrows at us from their happy little huddle. "What the fuck is this?" I was angry, of course, but more so I was inexplicably afraid. I wasn't sure that my fear was warranted—I wasn't in danger, I was surrounded by people. My fear felt irrational, and I didn't want him to see it.

Louis leaned forward, rested his elbows on his knees, and held his clasped hands towards me. He was still smiling. He spoke softly, imploring, "Lynn, I'm simply trying to tell you that this is why I have such difficulty in relationships. I was so deeply affected by what I saw. I was only a little boy."

I again glanced over at his wife, searching her posture for signs of meekness or fear that would help me decided whether this guy was for real or not. She was talking and laughing with her group.

"That day has stayed with me my whole life," he was saying, "the image of that woman's blood turning the dirt beneath her into mud. I can never forget it." His voice cracked. He looked as though he might cry.

I was torn. On the one hand, his story was obviously disturbing, but on the other hand, maybe I shouldn't assume that he was a staunch defender of some bullshit old-school code. I remembered what we'd all been learning how to do in this class. The active listening, the suspension of value judgments. We were supposed to be role playing. I looked into his eyes and tried to imagined a scared little boy who had stood helplessly by as a man savagely beat his naked wife in the street, in front of her own wailing children. What would that do to a little kid?

I looked at Susan and Anne for help. I couldn't remember who was supposed to mediating this pretend dispute. They both stared at Louis, mouths ajar.

"Louis," I said, abandoning my role as his co-disputant and trying to de-escalate whatever this was. "That must have been awful. You must have been so scared." Anne and Susan, on cue, murmured their sympathy, all of our previous fear and judgment vapourized by his show of vulnerability.

"Yes," said Louis, his voice morose, his eyes bigger and sadder than any other eyes I'd ever seen. "And that is why I cannot trust my wife now." My face froze, and my fists clenched reflexively. "A man breaks his back for his wife and his children," he continued. "And that man must remain vigilant, always. If my wife ever compromises me like that, she will feel in her bones the betrayal I will feel in my heart."

An airless cone of tension thumped down on our group of fives. I could not breathe. I could not speak. I could not take my eyes from Louis to see Susan's or Anne's reactions.

Marge appeared and broke the ringing in my ears by asking, "Is everything okay here?" She was smiling, but I could see she'd noticed the chill—how could she not?

"Yes, ma'am," said Louis, friendly and warm. His eyes stayed locked on mine. "This has been a particularly helpful exercise." Marge waited a beat. I could see her watching me, but I didn't trust myself enough to repeat what had just happened without bawling like an idiot, which is what I tended to do when I got mad. It wasn't so much what Louis had said that had me so upset—it was the fact that I'd given him the benefit of the doubt.

I thought about all the times I had been similarly suckered. Little things: like at work, when I'd leaned over the bar to try and catch a customer's order only to see him look down my shirt. Or on the street, trying to be helpful to men asking for directions, only to have them tell me I should smile more. Or, okay, there's bigger things, too. Worse things. Like when you suspect a guy might have a problem, but it's possible you're just reading him wrong, and you decide you can roll with it. And you do, at first, until it stops working, but by then you're deep in it and you're asking yourself, how the fuck did you not see this coming? Which is what had happened to me. Which is why I'm single and will be for the foreseeable future. Which is probably why Angela was so insistent that I join her in this course, and why I was so resistant.

All of this was whizzing through my head as I considered how to tell Marge what was happening. I imagined Louis sitting there, calm and in control of himself, while I made a scene explaining how he'd made me feel violated. If I spoke up and told her the truth, I would be upset, and he would be fine. But we were supposed to be acting. So I acted.

"Lynn," asked Marge, "is everything all right?"

I took a deep breath. I broke Louis's gaze and turned towards Marge. "Yes," I said in a steady voice. "Fine, thanks." She lingered a second longer, scanning my fake smile, but I gave her nothing.

She moved on and clapped her hands together, calling out that it was time to switch roles. "Everybody! Time to switch it up!"

The room filled with the drone of inane conversation and bodies in motion. I waited until Marge's back was turned and Angela was busy sharing a joke with her sixes, and then I hauled back and slapped Louis in the face so hard that I grunted with the exertion—so hard that the palm of my hand felt as though it split open on impact.

Louis said, "Ungh."

Susan cried out.

I heard a collective gasp, and my chair clattered onto its back as I bolted out of it. I slipped through the door and broke into a frantic run. Down the hallway, out the front doors, and into the night—I ran. It wasn't until I'd zig-zagged off the bright, crowded sidewalks of Bloor, through a graffitied laneway and onto a quiet residential street, that I recognized the sound of my feet pounding the pavement and stopped running.

I collapsed onto a bench in a small parkette and tried to get a handle on my ragged breathing. The square was quiet and dark. When I stopped feeling like I was going to have a heart attack, I paced around for a bit, cradling my throbbing hand. My mind wheeled—at what Louis had said, how I'd reacted. I'd never even yelled at anyone before. I'd certainly never hit anyone before. It hurt more than I thought it would. I had thought in the moment that I'd feel some rush of victory or triumph. Presumably, the man in Louis' story felt powerful while he was beating his wife. Presumably Louis felt powerful when he upset us women by telling that story. I just felt disoriented, like I didn't know what to do next.

The evening dew had dampened my Converse and the cuffs of my jeans. I wanted to kneel down to press my hot hands into the cool grass. Instead, I headed back towards Bloor to try to figure out where I was, and how to get home.

COREY WAS A DANGER CAT

COREY WAS A DANGER CAT. He was six guns wide and fit to kill. He had two pistols and a bleeding rosebud etched in felt marker on the flesh of his forearm. It was the mark of a hero wounded in love, he said. But he'd never tell about it.

"What's done is done," he'd say, and he'd shield his eyes from an imaginary sun as though he was looking for something. He'd seen that move on TV. It had made his heart feel hollow with understanding.

In the confines of his helmet, Corey's ears throbbed with the racket of the gravel grinding and popping under his plastic wheels. He no longer fit his Big Wheel properly, but it didn't matter. He's a Renaissance man. With shields up and rockets flaring, he pedaled flat-out, knees battering the chin-guard of his helmet, his elbows sticking out and back like shark fins. Like switchblades. No—like samurai swords.

His hollow wheels amplified the noise of the concrete slabs of the sidewalk—th-THUD, th-THUD, th-THUD— like jungle drums, or like the music that signals the approach of the hero when the bad guy least expects him. The noise had an effect on Corey that was simultaneously hypnotic and stimulating. His eyes grew wide and un- blinking: he became Corey the Danger Cat. He was ready, and it was time.

He sped north on Glenmore Avenue towards the first branch of his tripartide Saturday morning Axis of Evil. At 565 Glenmore, the Danger Cat slammed on his brakes and skidded sideways in a wide, well-practised arc across the driveway of Chantelle Peters, who sat on her front porch with Erin and Marnie Valentine. Marnie, who wasn't pretty, but was the most popular of the three because, or so Corey heard, she would show her boobs behind the dumpster out back of Mac's Milk in exchange for packs of KOOLs. They were sitting on Chantelle's porch sucking Pepsi Blue through straws they'd made from cherry Twizzlers with the ends chewed off. They did their best to pretend that he wasn't there, but their giggles betrayed them.

The Danger Cat threw back his head and screamed, "Let freedom reign! Let freedom *REIGN*!"

"Jerk," Chantelle said, sounding bored.

The Danger Cat registerd this as a victory, and shot down the sidewalk without looking back to witness the admiration he was certain he'd see in the other girls' eyes. He pumped his legs as fast as he could and tore a strip up Parklawn Boulevard, towards the second branch in his Axis of Evil.

At the corner of Parklawn and Franklin, the Danger Cat executed a one-eighty at the precise point at which Ru-Ru, the Bromowitzes' schnauzer, who'd come barrelling down the driveway at the sound of his approach, was abruptly choked back mid-air by the chain that kept her anchored to the porch. Poised like a panther surrounded by spear-wielding jungle midgets, the Danger Cat waited. His tongue darted up to indulge in the slippery salt that ran from his nose holes. His eyes shot from the Bromowitzes' screen door to their rose bushes, in which Mrs. Bromowitz was known to lurk, and back to Ru-Ru, who was going ballistic a mere three inches from the Danger Cat's tender but indifferent calf. Ru-Ru was mental, but Danger Cat was a coiled King Cobra, cool and slick. In the treetops, the Vikings wet their pants in fear, like fat babies who didn't know anything about being men. Corey was a man. Corey was a Danger Cat.

"Any minute now," thought the Danger Cat. "Any...freakin'...minute..."

"Corey Jackson!" Mrs. Bromowitz and her wooden spoon suddenly lurched towards the screen door from the darkened bowels of her lair. "I'm gonna call your mother! I mean it, I'm gonna call—"

The Danger Cat unleashed the voice of a thousand hounds of hell and shrieked, "Let freedom reign, Mrs. Bromowitz!"

"Ru-Ru, come!" Mrs. Bromowitz tugged at Ru-Ru's chain, but Ru-Ru was busy drowning the Danger Cat's message in frantic braying.

"Let freedom reign!"

"Corey, you're a brute!"

He was off like a bat from a cannonball bed, down Parklawn, down Glenmore, obliterating anthill after anthill after anthill. Past the porch where the girls were no longer sitting, but he hardly even noticed, because Danger Cat would one day see the boobs of every girl. Until then, he would fill up every anthill with water till crunchy ant corpses littered the earth like sprinkles on a doughnut.

The Danger Cat built up brain-bending speed travelling south on Glenmore, until the sidewalk cracks thumped against his tires in unison with the pounding of his knees against his helmet. Dead ahead, in Glenmore Square, he spied the third and most volatile branch in the Axis of Evil.

Cornchips sat, unaware of his fate, with his feet soaking in Glenmore's memorial fountain, mumbling to himself and picking gnats out of his long beard. The heat in the Danger Cat's helmet was like a supernova. A lesser man might have chosen to wait until the sun was lower in the sky, or he might have even called off the whole mission, but not the Danger Cat. He narrowed his eyes and forged ahead, nerves jangling and guns blazing.

When the Danger Cat was only a couple of feet away from the fountain, Cornchips looked up, smiled his hideously toothless smile, and cooed, "Here, kitty, kitty, kitty!" He doubled over with laughter. "Kitty Cat," he gasped. "C'mere, kitty, kitty!"

Disarmed, but determined, Corey drove his Big Wheel in tight circles around the fountain until the juice in his head began to swirl. He drove into a flock of pigeons and braked to watch them scatter into a whirling circle above his head.

"That dog get you yet, puss-puss?" Cornchips asked.

"It's *Danger* Cat," Corey said over his shoulder.

It was cool in the shade by the fountain. Cornchips seemed unusually docile, so Corey reckoned he had some time before the action started. He allowed himself to be temporarily distracted by a fresh puddle of pigeon shit. He nudged his Big Wheel forward until his front wheel made contact with it. Then he slowly reversed until he could see the splotch on his tire. Corey turned his front wheel slightly to the left and inched forward again, testing his poop stamp on a clean bit of pavement. It worked. Corey eyed the rest of the concrete around the fountain and wondered how much he could accomplish before the poop dried.

"I'm not a fan of spinach, myself," Cornchips said. Corey was used to this out-of-nowhere talk, and ignored it, biding his time, absorbing himself in making poop stamps. Corey flinched as Cornchips stood up, but Cornchips merely bent over to pick a yellowed cigarette butt out of a crevice in the concrete at the edge of the fountain. He ran it under his nose like a fine cigar, and then jammed it between his cracked lips, patting down his pockets for a light.

"I mean, I'll eat it if it's *on* something," he continued. "Like a pizza or what have you, but I'm not exactly over the *moon* for it."

Cornchips struck a sputtering match, held it to the mashed end of the cigarette, and puffed madly. When the embers at the end of the cigarette failed to catch, he swore under his breath and spat the butt into the fountain. That's when Cornchips turned to face Corey, who was admiring the arc of white splotches he'd made with his wheel.

"Boy!"

Corey tensed at the edge in Cornchips' voice. He placed his feet on his pedals and squeezed his tasseled handgrips.

Their eyes locked. They stared at each other in silence. They both knew what was coming.

Corey took a slow, deep breath.

"Don't you try it, boy," Cornchips warned. He rolled up his right sleeve without taking his eyes off Corey, revealing a pale green smudge that had been, in his youth, a bold tattoo on his once-muscular forearm. "I'm warning you..."

Corey licked his lips.

"So help me god..." said Cornchips. His right hand slowly disappeared into his right pocket.

It was now or never—the old man's reflexes were slow, and Corey knew it.

"Letfreedomreign!" he blurted and then peeled away from the fountain in a spray of pebbles and pigeon poop, his eyes wild, his legs pumping like pistons.

The water splashed up over the sides of the fountain's basin as Cornchips lurched in Corey's direction.

"What business is that of yours!" Cornchips screamed, and hurled a peach pit at Corey's helmet. THOCK! A direct hit. Corey's front wheel wobbled slightly, and then corrected itself.

Cornchips crowed with pleasure. "Take that, you little shit!"

"Let freedom reign!" Corey yelled once more over his shoulder. He glimpsed Cornchips struggling to climb out of the fountain and knew he'd go root around in the grass for his peach pit.

After about a block of flat-out pedaling, the wind whistling past his helmet vents and the squirrels running for cover, Corey let out the breath he'd been holding. Elated, he threw back his head and howled. He could do anything and go anywhere, and he would do it all with his head held high. He would look people in the eye. He'd gone up against the whole stinking Axis of Evil and not a single one of them had flung the usual insult at him. The word that the school kids yelled at him through the chain-link fence where he and the other kids like him had their separate recesses, the word that made his mother cry till his Nana snapped, "Cry alls you want, Belinda, but it ain't gonna make him right."

Today there'd be no lonely skulking on his driveway, watching the other kids play. Today was a day for sidewalks and shopping malls and schoolyards and all the other places in which he ordinarily hung his head. Today he'd shown them all. He was six guns wide and fit to kill. Corey was a Danger Cat.

ESTEEM

ON SATURDAY, the day of her daughter's Grade 1 ballet exam, Susan woke up early, sick with nerves. She slipped out of bed without disturbing Dan and went downstairs to fix breakfast for the kids. At the kitchen counter, her hands darted through their tasks by rote, leaving her mind free to tally the various chores she had to tend to before the exam. Lay out clothes for the kids. Get Dan to dress Trevor. Feed them all lunch. Bathe Alison. Get Alison dressed and ready. Pack Alison's gym bag with her leotard, ballet slippers, and snacks for the car. Get herself dressed and ready. She sighed and called the kids to the table, mindful of Dan still sleeping above them. While Alison lobbed Cheerios at her captivated little brother, Susan worked in silence, polishing the kitchen sink to a blinding shine, which helped—a little—to quell her nausea.

She kept an eye on Alison as she chattered away to her brother, seemingly oblivious to the challenge that lay ahead of her. Susan felt a warm swell of pride. Alison was only seven—too young to fully appreciate the pressure of a ballet exam—so Susan had accepted the burden of anxiety on her daughter's behalf.

Susan had met Dan seven years ago. She'd been a night student at a hair school. She planned to rent a chair as soon as she graduated, and to save so that in a few years she'd be able to open her own salon. But as it turned out, doing hair was not as glamourous as she'd imagined when she was a kid watching *CityLine* makeovers. She was forever scratching away other people's hair clippings, which somehow showed up in her socks, the waistband of her underwear, and her bra. Her hands were dry and cracked from the constant washing, and her nails discoloured from the dyes. And when she wasn't working or taking classes, she was standing around the hallways of the community college with handmade flyers offering free practice haircuts.

That's how she'd met Dan. He was in auto mechanics. She'd done his hair back when she was trying to learn fades. He hadn't said a word through the whole ordeal, not even when Susan's teacher had slapped Susan's hands away while she tried to fix Susan's mistakes. At the end of the cut, Dan had leaned forward in his chair, scrutinized each side of his head in the mirror, said "good enough," and asked for her phone number. Ecstatic, Susan thought he wanted to book another appointment. When she realized he just wanted a date, she was still pleased. He'd been nice, after all, when most customers wouldn't have missed an opportunity to be self-righteously critical.

In Susan's mind, Dan was basically rich. Had he not been so introverted, his dating prospects might have been better, in which case Susan might have been out of luck. But Susan later learned that by the time Dan asked for her number, he'd already struck out with everyone else. One of the women he'd dated was in her hair school and confided that he didn't like going out and wasn't particularly fun to hang out with or interesting to talk to. Susan figured she could handle that—she couldn't afford to go anywhere, and could never think of anything interesting to say, anyway.

Susan always thought they'd made an awkward couple. She was three inches taller than Dan, with broad shoulders and dark, lank hair; he was fair and petite. They had little in common, but she knew that getting married to someone in the city was her best shot at staying there—and then she got pregnant with Alison. At first, she hadn't wanted to keep the baby, but having a kid with Dan, and accepting the help from his parents, seemed like the safe bet. Dan had shrugged when she asked if he wanted this, the baby, and by extension, her.

"Will you stay, though?" she'd asked him. "Even if you later you regret it?"

"I will if you want me to," he'd said.

Susan pulled a box of Jell-O from the pantry to make dessert after lunch. Green. Alison's favourite. She was very careful about Alison's diet. As she plugged the kettle in, she reflected on all that she and Dan had accomplished. Two kids, a new house in a new subdivision courtesy of the mortgage they'd qualified for when Dan was hired at the plant. His parents agreed to co-sign and help with the down payment. Her own parents had never helped her like that. They weren't mean about it, they just had no money. They only visited once, when she and Dan first brought Alison home from the hospital. Her father had bought Dan a bottle of Crown Royal. Susan still had the velveteen bag tucked away in a box with Alison's baby clothes. Nowadays Susan called her mother on Sunday afternoon and they'd talk about *Coronation Street*. The new machinist at Underworld, Karen McDonald, was stirring things up.

"I like her," Susan said. "She's tall."

"Doesn't hide the extra weight."

"Alison's exam is in a few weeks. You should come down."

"We'll see."

Susan's mother always hung up first.

Dan was watching WWE the living room. The ballet exam was at four. As if the very premise of an exam wasn't daunting enough, the exam was in Toronto. Susan was afraid to drive in the city. She hadn't even had a driver's license until she met Dan, but he'd taught her how to drive out on the concessions north of Oshawa. Traffic and narrow streets were not her strong suit. Besides, without Dan's presence in Toronto, Susan would have felt vulnerable to the muttering homeless people sprawled across the sewer grates who sometimes yelled at passersby. Or the squeegee-ers under the Gardiner Expressway. Or the beggars who approached the car at stoplights asking for change, their grubby faces and handwritten pleas for help looming in her peripheral vision as she pretended not to see them. She had eventually convinced Dan to drive, which was worth all the arguing because it killed two birds with one stone: she wouldn't have to navigate the streets that teemed with traffic and impatient people, and Alison would never know that Dan didn't actually want to go to her exam.

Dan seemed to tolerate the kids well enough, even if he wasn't particularly engaged with them. He'd stuck around, like he said he would. He paid the bills. Susan had thought that with time, they would grow closer, be more like how she imagined a married couple might be if they weren't messed up. It could have been better. Susan buried her disappointment by imagining that everything she did for Alison, from the ballet classes to the green Jell-O, would cement their mother-daughter bond, make it something she'd never had. Her and Alison would be different. Better.

It seemed like Susan had only just finished cleaning up from breakfast and lunch when it was time to get ready. Alison hadn't wanted any of the Jell-O, so Susan gulped it down before dashing upstairs. She ran a bath for Alison, making sure that Alison's favourite toys lined the tub and the pink bubble bath was foaming appropriately. She then removed her own dress from its plastic dry-cleaning shell, hung it from the top of her bathroom door, and stepped back to admire it. Susan smiled, imagining the look of surprised appreciation in Dan's eyes as he watched her float down the staircase in the wispy cloud of fabric. Susan had stopped at The Bay yesterday and splurged on expensive control-top pantyhose and a new pair of shoes. Shoes with a hint of a heel—a departure from her usual flats, but ultimately necessary. No one need judge her daughter by the sensible flats of her suburban mother. Dan would be proud to walk into the ballet school with her on his arm, and Alison would be proud to have a pretty mother.

Susan's own mother had been darker, moodier, than all of the other mothers she'd met. She knew that her mother spent time in foster care, but that was about all she knew. It wasn't something they talked about. In the weeks leading up to Susan's wedding, while she hunted for a wedding dress that camouflaged her baby bump, she'd sent suggestions to her mother for a suitable mother-of-the-bride outfit. Susan wasn't surprised when her mother showed up at Toronto's City Hall in a Kmart special, carrying her usual purse like it was just another day.

They spent their one-night honeymoon at the Westin Harbour Castle in Toronto. She'd imagined a lake view, but their room faced a condo. They'd looked up the prices of the food in the hotel and decided instead to order in their usual from Pizza Pizza. They were eating in bed. Dan had brought a cooler of beer from home. Occasionally, from the hallway, Susan could hear people laughing as they headed out for the evening. Susan wondered where they were going, and how they could afford it.

"Our kid will be better than us, Dan," she'd said.

Dan was peeling the corner of the label off of his bottle of Budweiser. "I'm doing fine, thanks."

"Don't you want more than this?" she said, waving one hand in an arc above the empty pizza box and the Doritos bag on the bedspread.

"I don't know what you're on about, but look around— no one's stopping you."

"Well I can't do much else if I'm having your child, can I?"

Dan shrugged and kept his eyes on the TV. "Suit yourself," he said.

Susan tended to Alison's hair. They were already running behind schedule, and the Jell-O taste in Susan's throat was acrid. Alison had grown quiet, and sat perfectly still on the toilet lid while Susan, dressed only in her underwear, bra, and pantyhose, brushed out Alison's long, blond hair. She had a special hairspray for Alison's hair, one that gave the surface of the hair follicle a shimmery, brightening effect. She'd seen an ad for it in one of the trade magazines that she still subscribed to.

"Do you see this pretty lady's hair, sweetheart?" she'd asked Alison, pushing the magazine across the dinner table a few weeks ago during dinner. Alison shrugged. She was picking up Dan's annoying habits.

"Would you like Mommy to give you pretty hair like that for your ballet exam?" Alison shrugged again and turned her attention back to dinner plate. "Wouldn't you like your hair to be prettier than all the other little girls?" Susan asked. Alison had smiled and said sure.

"Do you see what I got for you, sweetheart? Just like you wanted."

She showed Alison the hairspray bottle, which was covered in glittering starbursts. "Remember how you said you wanted Mommy to get you this?"

Alison studied the bottle but said nothing.

"That's okay. Mommy doesn't mind doing extra things for her special girl."

Alison smiled up at her. "Thank you, Mommy."

"You're welcome."

Susan gestured at her dress on the back of the door. "Do you see Mommy's dress? Isn't it pretty?"

"Vewy pwetty." said Alison.

Susan bristled at the Alison's pronunciation. It was something she'd begged Dan to help fix by paying for the speech therapy lessons Alison's school had recommended. Dan had refused because his mother insisted Alison would grow out of it on her own.

"Ve*r*y pretty, Alison. Pay attention to your *R* sounds. You have lots of p*r*etty d*r*esses, don't you? Can you tell Mommy about your p*r*etty d*r*esses?"

Alison nodded.

"Don't move your head, honey, Mommy's doing your hair."

Susan adored brushing and braiding Alison's hair. So blond it was almost white, Susan could lose herself entirely in its cool waves of refracted light. Susan had made a little look book for Alison's ballet hairstyles. This was something she'd learned in school—stylists kept scrapbooks of their inspirations and accomplishments. She would take a picture of Alison's hair when she was done and add it to the book. If she ever returned to hairstyling, she would have a look book ready to go—provided she could fill the pages with decent work.

Susan contemplated Alison's silence. Gone was the precocious little girl who had babbled away at breakfast. She tried to soothe Alison's nerves while she braided her hair.

"You're lucky to be so petite and blond," Susan murmured. "You make such a beautiful ballerina. And look at your tiny little feet."

Susan's shoes were a size eleven, bigger than Dan's. Alison clearly took after him. Dan reminded her of that—the shoes and the genes—on a regular basis.

"I was so big when I was growing up," Susan continued, "that I always felt like a moose compared to the other little girls."

Alison wrinkled her nose and said, "Mummy, will I be big?"

Stung, Susan sucked in her breath and reflexively yanked Alison's braid tighter, pulling at the hair she'd brushed back from Alison's temples until the tender flesh there was raised like goose pimples. Alison's eyes watered and her brow wrinkled, but she didn't protest. Instead, she closed her eyes. Susan felt a pang of guilt and told Alison how beautiful she was. Alison didn't respond.

When Susan was satisfied with arranging Alison's hair on top of her head in an elaborate knot of tiny individual braids, her arms and hands ached and her feet were sore from standing on the linoleum. Alison seemed glum and withdrawn.

"Go get yourself dressed, Alison." She steered Alison out into the hall towards her room. "Your dress and shoes are laid on your bed. Be careful with your hair. Hurry up, okay?"

Susan took the dress from the back of the bathroom door and hurried to get dressed. She'd spent too much time on Alison's hair and had fallen even further behind. She could hear Dan downstairs, making a big production of opening the front hall closet and pulling out his shoes. She could hear Trevor downstairs, too. She hoped that Dan had at least gotten Trevor dressed. Susan was always running late, and Dan was always making a point of being punctual. The later Susan was, the angrier Dan got. This had become a ritual, and because they never left the house without it, they now rarely left the house together.

Susan struggled to close the clasp on her dress, and this set off a series of hateful observations about her appearance. Her pores were huge, her eyelids drooped, and she hated the dress, too. It barely fit her. She had put on weight since she'd last had an excuse to wear it. It had been over a year—she should have known better. She should have bought a new dress. She had no backup plan.

Dan yelled up the stairs at her to pick up the pace. Exasperated, Susan grabbed her makeup and her jewellery, and tossed it all loose into her purse. She would have to put on the finishing touches in the car. The front door slammed as she ran a brush through her hair one last time. Downstairs, she found the house empty. She peered through the curtains and saw that Dan had backed the car down the driveway and was idling at the curb in front of the house.

Susan got in the car and laughingly commented on how cold it was, hoping to cut the tension with small talk instead of inviting Dan's usual tirade by apologizing. He ignored her and pulled away from the curb. Susan turned in her seat to check on Alison.

"Don't rest you head against the seat, honey. You'll muss your hair."

Alison wordlessly tilted her head forward to stare at her hands in her lap.

"Thatta girl. We won't be too long in the car."

The four of them sat in silence for the one-hour drive into the city.

It was January and bitterly cold downtown. Columns of steam slanted up from the manhole covers and the asphalt was white with salt stains. Wind whipped Susan's face and her eyes watered as they walked towards the ballet school. She felt guilty about exposing Alison's little head to the cold, but a hat or hood would ruin her hair. It really was only a short walk. Susan dabbed her eyes with a tissue, worried about her makeup, and tried her best to avoid the patches of ice on the sidewalks. She'd made sure Dan had put the children in their snowsuits, even though she knew Alison would have whined about it, but Susan had worn only her faux-leather dress coat. It wasn't lined, and was therefore quite slimming, but it had frozen stiff in the wind and seemed to amplify the cold. Her pantyhose did nothing to keep the sting from her legs, and she could feel the blisters forming from her new shoes.

Dan was clearly furious with her, and she couldn't blame him. They were late, on this day that was so important for Alison. He plowed ahead, carrying Trevor in one arm and holding Alison's hand in the other. Susan lagged behind, carrying Alison's gym bag. She was used this—feeling like she'd let them down. She was the weak link in the family chain. Susan huffed as she tried to keep up.

Dan barked something over his shoulder at her, something about the address, and as Susan rummaged through her purse for her phone, she hit a patch of ice and her shoes slipped out from beneath her. She cried out, flung her arms wide, and then crashed down on her back. She struggled to catch the breath that had shot from her lungs as she hit the concrete.

Dan and Alison glanced back at the sound of her impact. Susan raised her head, seeking Dan's help, but what she saw in his eyes crushed her.

Alison started giggling. "Mommy get up, you silly!"

"Susan, get up," echoed Dan.

Susan rocked side to side, trying to right herself. But her jacket was too tight and her breath wouldn't come. She waved her arms up towards Dan, but he made no move to help her.

"My hands are full. Get up."

Now Trevor and Alison were both giggling.

"Get up, silly Mommy," Trevor mimicked Alison, with glee.

Susan's head fell back against the pavement and her arms dropped still at her sides. Rivulets of mascara ran across her temples and into her hair. She tilted her head back, her mouth open, and tried again to catch her breath.

Alison was now fully in the grips of a giggle fit.

"Mommy, you silly moose!" she crowed with delight.

A wave of shame tore through Susan with such ferocity that her breath filled her lungs in a series of spasms. She exhaled in a long, plaintive sob that reverberated off the buildings surrounding them.

Trevor stopped giggling, and Alison gasped and looked up at Dan, who was staring stone-faced at Susan.

"What's wong with Mommy?" asked Alison in a small voice.

Dan swore under his breath, turned on his heel, and pulled impatiently at Alison's hand. Alison allowed herself to be lead away, but continued to look back over her shoulder at her mother, who lay weeping on the sidewalk, the contents of her purse strewn across the grimy asphalt, twinkling like stardust in the early glow of the street lights.

THE MOUTHS OF BABES

IN THE SUMMER between first and second grade, I dared Becky Morton to eat the dog turd we'd found on the Griffins' front lawn.

It was late afternoon. Summer. The sun shone warm and sleepy on the nutty sausage at our feet. I sat down opposite Becky. My little sister and another kid from up the street flanked us. We stared with quiet intensity at the textured coil between us, as though waiting for it to speak up and object to my reckless dare on Becky's behalf.

I'd lodged the dare in the spirit of carefree abandon, but it hung heavy in the air, loaded with the weight of its implications. My words seemed suspended just beyond my lips. Their lingering evoked in Becky the kind of resignation she needed to pull off this stunt like the seasoned meeter-of-dares she claimed to be. Sadly, that was the only card Becky had to play in the complex social labyrinth of our youth: self-destruction. Her Kool-Aid-ringed mouth, stringy hair, and the sour milk smell that clung to her clothes rendered her different, unlikable. But she was brave, and she usually did what we told her to do. We liked that.

Becky bought herself some time by pointing out the logistical flaw of my dare. In my excitement, I had not included any terms that required Becky to actually *touch* the turd, which she was loath to do, as its surface looked "icky." I, feeling defensive of my oversight and not wanting my dare to lose momentum, quickly handed Becky a serving twig and went back to holding my breath.

Becky then pointed out that the stick had been on the ground and so was not hygienic enough to employ as an eating utensil.

My sister and I took the twig from Becky's grimy hand and carefully peeled back the bark. We explained as we did so that the tender green surface beneath the bark had long been known to bushmen and schoolchildren alike as a perfectly hygienic utensil, primarily used for roasting marshmallows, but easily adapted for other cuisines. I handed the peeled switch back to Becky. Her silence indicated she'd reached the end of her stalling. We leaned forward, four sunburnt heads nearly touching, as the cicadas filled the air with shrill notes of caution.

Becky licked her lips and gave the coil an exploratory pat with the end of her switch. It cut the turd easily in two, rounding the edges like a dull butter knife would cleave a bran muffin. "You're lucky, Becky," I whispered. "Looks like you won't have to chew."

Becky drew the twig towards her and peered suspiciously at the matter clinging to its tip. It was now or never. She held the stick so close that I feared her next breath would draw her attention to the stink, breaking the tenuous spell of my influence.

"You said you'd do it, Becky. We're all waiting."

She moved like lightning. In less than a second, Becky had stuck out her tongue and run it up the business end of her stick, and then flung the stick to the ground. We all began to scream in revulsion and disbelief.

She was stuck—her tongue hanging out, dog shit sliding down its moist, pebbled surface to pool at its tip. She began to scream with the rest of us, no doubt just as horrified by her actions as we were. But with her tongue out of her mouth, screaming proved difficult, and at best she could only manage a nasal "Euu..." sound, which did nothing to assuage her mortification. Thwarted, Becky bolted to her feet and fled across the sun-dappled lawn into the quiet sanctity of her neighbouring home, where she was safe from the frenzied shrieks of her former friends—us.

I've often wondered about the sequence of events that took place after she'd entered the house. Was her mother there? Of course she was. I remember her always staring, trance-like, out the kitchen window at nothing in particular while she idly stirred a pitcher of Kool-Aid. Did she know then that the Kool-Aid was the only reason we let Becky play with us?

Had Becky's mother seen what happened? Or had Becky simply grabbed the first thing she saw when she ran into the kitchen—a dishtowel—and rubbed her tongue raw with it? Would her mother have even noticed?

What transpired later, when Becky's mother discovered the offending dishtowel folded neat as a pin over the handle of the oven, inexplicably smeared with feces? Would she have demanded an explanation? Maybe Becky's mother knew that feces on a neatly folded dishtowel could only mean a fall from grace, and that maintaining one's dignity in such circumstances required a bit of mystery. Maybe Becky's mother, without saying a word, hid the dishtowel under the potato peels in the garbage bin and returned to the task before her: stirring yet another lurid pitcher of Kool-Aid for Becky and her friends.

THIS KEEPS HAPPENING

KARLA IS DRIFTING OFF TO SLEEP. She lets her body melt into the mattress and ignores the drool fanning out beneath the corner of her mouth. A long, low rumble begins to spill from her sinuses when two words jolt her awake: *You're dying!*

This keeps happening. Each time she's startled and lies there, bug-eyed and rigid in her bed, mentally scanning her body for signs of terminal illness—aches or cramps that she might have otherwise dismissed. Each time she finds nothing.

Karla is not sure whether she is actually dying; at least, no more so than anyone else. But she read somewhere that death is preceded by premonition. If that's the case, Karla figures this is about as clear as premonitions get.

Karla is young—thirty-five—so she shouldn't be dying yet, even if her life is pretty dull. But because she's so certain that her time is up, she has decided to try and embrace the reality of imminent death. She tells herself that there is freedom in it, and she tries to enjoy the windfall of her shifting priorities.

She sits up on the edge of the mattress, resolving to ignore the sight of her clothes strewn across the bedroom floor, as though dragged there by receding floodwaters. She shuffles to the bathroom, squinting at the light and lifting her toes off the cold tiles. From the toilet, she eyes the black footprints in the tub and the orange ribbon of rust that runs down its lip from the stopper's chain. She finishes up in the bathroom and wades through the unopened mail that litters the hallway to the kitchen. She excavates a space among the dirty dishes in the sink so she can fill the kettle, and turns on the stove's back burner.

"People will think that I've always lived like this," she muses, watching the stovetop filament turn from dark red to bright orange.

To address this very concern about her domestic reputation, Karla has prepared a note for Edward, the superintendent—she knows he's the one most likely to find her bloated remains slumped over on the couch beneath a pizza box or, more likely, moldering in her bed beneath the duvet. The note, typed up on her computer and printed in triplicate, reads *Please be advised: Whereas ordinarily, I'm immaculate, whereas I suspected I was dying, let it be known that I chose not to go out cleaning.*

She's taped the note to the mirror in the front hall. It's in a Ziploc bag, because she read about a body that went undiscovered in an un-air-conditioned apartment like hers for several days during a heat wave, until the body exploded, soiling everything within spattering range. The Ziploc bag also holds her emergency contacts and an urgent plea: should she be found face down on the bathroom floor with a fistful of toilet paper, Karla does not wish to be resuscitated.

"How long do premonitions continue before they come true?" Karla wonders as the stovetop element bursts into flame and the crumbs from yesterday's toast go up in smoke. "I can't avoid cleaning forever."

She blows out the fire, fans the smoke away from the smoke detector with a crusty tea towel, and despairs at the state of her kitchen. The recycling she's stopped putting to the curb has begun to collect in the corners like brittle snowdrifts. Her fridge is barren but for a squat, economy-sized jar of Maille Dijon—a smug yellow idol in a shrine of frosted white light.

"They'll think I really liked mustard." She considers revising her letter to the superintendent. *Whereas the mustard was there when I moved in.*

She waits for the kettle to boil and distracts herself from the urge to clean by contemplating the ramifications of her impending death. There aren't any, aside from the tragic loss, sure to be felt on a global scale, of the novel Karla has contemplating for the past ten years. She has yet to commit a single word of her masterpiece to paper and is therefore confident of its brilliance. Karla also knows that all the instructors in all the creative writing classes in the world can't teach brilliance.

"You either get it," as Karla has so often chanted to her reflection, "or you don't." Luckily, Karla gets it—comes by it quite naturally, in fact—and is therefore not remotely interested in bettering herself or her latent talent through personal or professional development.

So sure had she been of her latent literary brilliance that she had not pursued a degree or any other path to stable employment. Instead, while she waited for someone to discover her talent, she spent her twenties moving from one job to the next, nurturing certain eccentricities that she believed would endear her to her future fans, and make her portrayal in her posthumous biopic an especially rewarding challenge for Meryl Streep. A side effect of all these eccentricities is her alienation her from her family, friends, and colleagues. She stares intently at people from under her brow, which she carefully arranges each morning into deep furrows. It helps that she needs glasses but can't afford them. She pretends to be enormously disappointed in everything, all the time, which frankly is not much of a stretch. She is vocal and strident in her views, no matter how inconsequential the issue. She owns a pashmina. More recently, she had been practicing theatrical temper tantrums in her apartment. She had a mental list of customer service providers she could lay into in public if the spirit so moved her. She knows for example that she is free to degrade secretaries, personal support workers, chambermaids, house cleaners, and people who hand out the free *Daily Dispatch* at the city's main intersections and subway stations. Those people are hired to be thrown to the wolves; Karla knows this because she has held—and been fired from—each of those jobs over the course of the last year. She is still smarting over the most recent incident in which she was fired by the *Daily Dispatch* for simply holding her ground.

That morning in December, the morning she'd been fired, she'd been stationed outside of Sheppard–Yonge station where she handed out *Dispatches* to office workers who either snatched the paper out of her hand, ignored her, or told her to go fuck herself. Karla felt like she'd go mad from biting her tongue. At a quarter to ten, as she waited for someone to take the last paper of her shift, an old man trundled right up to her like a tank and started yelling at her about asset swaps.

She did not take the bait.

"Tell it to the Competition Bureau, sir," Karla said. She dropped the paper at his feet, turned on her heel, and walked into the subway station, cold and exhausted. Her face was chapped from the wind. As she was about to drop her token into the box at the ticket collector's booth, she tensed at an announcement: delay at Sheppard–Yonge station due to police investigation onboard a train. Northbound service suspended. Everyone around her groaned, but Karla felt like she'd won the TTC lottery. She was heading south. She dropped her token into the box and headed towards the stairs.

As she walked down the stairs to the subway platform, Karla hit a wall of people coming her way. She stood on her toes, craned her neck and saw a TTC guy clearing the southbound platform. She was immediately filled with rage. The announcement had been misleading! She'd already paid to get in! They'd have to reimburse her! She imagined unleashing one of her well-practiced tantrums on the ticket collector upstairs.

The TTC guy on the platform wouldn't answer when people asked him what was going on. Karla pressed forward against the crowd, thinking that if she could get within earshot, she could make him give her an answer, but the crowd was too thick. She was eventually pushed back up the stairs, where she latched onto the handrail and defiantly stood her ground as weary commuters trudged past her.

"I am not taking a shuttle bus all the way down to Bloor!" she yelled at no one in particular. "Are you kidding me?" She stood on her toes. "Those things are a nightmare!" she yelled over top of the crowd. "I'll wait right here, thanks!"

She looked around for solidarity. People seemed to be avoiding eye contact.

Suddenly, police officers were running past her and down the stairs to the now-empty platform. A lady behind Karla said in a weary voice, "Musta been somebody jumped, so's there's blood all over the platform."

Karla was distracted by the contrast between the crudeness of the woman's grammar and the cinematic quality of her imagination. This could be start of a story, she thought. Karla allowed her focus to drift away from the calamity in the subway station and into the process of bringing this woman's interior world onto the page—a world in which the human body has the structural integrity of ripe cantaloupe. A world in which a subway train would pull into a station at the speed of light such that a body on the tracks would erupt and spray blood across the subway platform like slop thrown from a bucket.

No, thought Karla. Scratch that. Karla didn't do magical realism, or whatever that was. Besides, erupting cantaloupe bodies would not play well on *Canada Reads*. Karla turned around to correct the woman's grammar and inform her that the blood would not, in fact, be "all over the platform," when another police officer—gun drawn—ran through the ticket turnstile and headed down the stairs.

The woman said, "Musta been a bomb scare."

Karla felt her own incredulity. She stared deep into the woman's makeup-smeared eyes, which were impenetrable, like those of a dumb animal.

"You're imagining that the officer will shoot his gun at the bomb?" Karla asked. "Have you literally no capacity for logical thought?"

"MOVE!" Karla looked up. A sweaty, red-faced officer with a bulletproof vest and an automatic rifle was running right at her. It was like a scene out of a movie. Karla mentally sketched out the stage directions: sweaty armed man runs past protagonist and down the stairs, subway passengers scream and scatter towards the exits while our protagonist remains resolute in her pursuit of accountability for public funds.

"Is this some kind of drill?" Karla yelled over one shoulder at the man in the ticket booth. The dumb woman behind her had disappeared. The Korean ladies who ran the accessory shop inside the subway station were wailing and trying to lower the security grate over their plate glass display window, but it wouldn't budge. One of them gave up and fled, crying as she ran towards the exit. The other lady curled up in a ball on the floor.

"Don't worry," Karla shouted. "The ticket collector is still sitting in the booth. You think he'd just be sitting there like that if his life was in danger? And listen, there's no noise coming up from the platform."

The lady seemed to consider this before she decided to bolt, too.

"There's nobody yelling on the platform!" Karla shouted at the woman's fleeing back. "They yell at people before they shoot them! This a false alarm! Or a training exercise! Which by the way," Karla turned back around to yell down the stairs, "is bullshit if you ask me, because they could do this at night when the subway isn't full of tired people who are just trying to LIVE THEIR LIVES!"

Karla was yelling so loud that her throat felt ragged and she was out of breath. The station was now completely empty except for Karla and the ticket collector, who was watching her from inside his booth. He slowly picked up a phone and spoke into it without taking his eyes off of her.

"Go ahead and call your goons!" Karla shouted at him. "I'm not leaving unless you reimburse me for my fare!"

A new automated announcement came over the intercom: service suspension both ways at Sheppard–Yonge station for a security incident. Karla tightened her grip on the banister. She was ready for a fight.

The TTC Constables did eventually escort her from the premises, but she went willingly, after she was satisfied she had impressed upon them the importance of punctuality and reliability to a successful transit system, and when she saw the shuttle buses were only going two stops down to where the subway service was still running. In all of the excitement, though, Karla had forgotten to remove her

Daily Dispatch smock. By the time she got home that afternoon, there was a message from her supervisor telling her not to come back to work, and instructing her on how to return her smock to head office or else they'd deduct the cost of it from her last paycheque. Karla shut off her ringer and went to bed for three days straight. The premonitions of her own death started when she woke up. That was three weeks ago.

The kettle boils, and Karla slowly pours the water over her tea bag—a morning habit that she'd curated in her twenties because it seemed like something a writer would do.

"Seems a shame it should all die with me," she whispers, watching her tea bag sink slowly to the bottom of her cup. Like her unwritten novel, which there was no point in starting, since she wouldn't have time finish it. And all the things she'd seen—things that would have formed the foundation of her book and its many sequels. She thinks of the boxes of notebooks she'd accumulated over the past ten years. On every birthday and Christmas, from every supportive, well-meaning relative and friend, back when they were still willing to put up with her. Moleskines. Floral hardcovers. Pocket-sized, letter-sized. Brand new and re-gifted. Some lined, some not. Some with calendars, some without. Monogrammed. Watermarked. Plain. All of them, empty.

A vision comes to her: an ending to her as-yet-unwritten novel. Edward, the superintendent, is in the building's dark and grimy basement. It's the height of summer. The basement is cool but humid. He groans as he shifts mildewed boxes from a storage locker onto a metal dolly. The rubber grips on the dolly's handles have disintegrated with time, leaving his hands smelling of pennies long after he's touched them.

He sighs and lifts the last box to the top of the pile on the dolly. He has already dumped four loads of these boxes into the garbage. This is the last. He slams the now empty storage-locker door shut behind him and the twang echoes down the damp concrete hallway.

"Edward?" the building manager hollers down the elevator shaft. "Edward! The police are here about unit 804!"

Edward runs through his mental roster of tenants most likely to die without anyone noticing. Karla. Karla what's-her-name is in 804. Her rent is two months overdue. He hasn't seen her since last winter, and she was clearly unhinged back then. He doesn't need the police to identify the stink at her end of the hallway. Edward nods in the dark. Good riddance; the woman was a bully.

He pushes his cart down the hall and prays that Karla what's-her-name had the decency to get rid of all her crap before she kicked the bucket. Edward enters the garbage room and pulls the dolly up to the open end of the Dumpster. He pulls at the packing tape that seals the box shut, flips open the top, and smirks at what he sees.

Stacks of lumpy notebooks huddle shoulder to shoulder, swaddled in yellowed newsprint. The pen on the thick covers has faded away completely, leaving only a cursive indentation. Edward runs his finger across the script. He picks up a notebook and considers reading it, then he shrugs and tosses the notebook into the Dumpster. If he'd had a dime for every mildewed box of pointless, self-obsessed vitriol he'd tossed, he wouldn't be stuck here, mopping up other people's messes for a living.

"The things I've seen," mutters Edward as he heaves the rest of the boxes into the dumpster. He shuts the door and trudges off to the elevator, dragging his heels as he goes.

"I could write a book."

CREDITS

Earlier versions of these stories have appeared in print:

"Corey Was a Danger Cat" and "The Princess Is Dead" in *Taddle Creek*

"Words for Evelyn" in *subTerrain*

"The Mouths of Babes" in *THIS Magazine*

"The Princess Is Dead" and "A Fare for Francis" as the chapbook *2 Stories*, published by Proper Tales Press

ACKNOWLEDGEMENTS

Stuart Ross, for 20+ years of friendship, patience, and guruship, thank you. I am grateful to those who encouraged me to write, including The Ladies Guild (but especially Laura Rantin), Daphne Boxhill, Harmony Toumai, June Croken, Inti Ali, Marco Landini, Heather Conklin, Digal Haio, Swathi Sehkar, Michelle Winters, Big D, but most especially and deeply, Matthew Smith. Shout-out to The Jacademy for Wayward Women and Girls and its Madam. Leigh Nash, your gentle guidance and tough questions made me a better writer. Thanks also to Alison Strobel for her eagle eyes and Megan Fildes for, really, the perfect cover. Thank you to the Arts Councils of Toronto and Ontario, and the taxpayers who fund them. Finally, very special thanks to my first love and muse, the City of Toronto and its people.

INVISIBLE PUBLISHING produces fine Canadian literature for those who enjoy such things. As an independent, not-for-profit publisher, our work includes building communities that sustain and encourage engaging, literary, and current writing.

Invisible Publishing has been in operation for over a decade. We released our first fiction titles in the spring of 2007, and our catalogue has come to include works of graphic fiction and nonfiction, pop culture biographies, experimental poetry, and prose.

We are committed to publishing diverse voices and experiences. In acknowledging historical and systemic barriers, and the limits of our existing catalogue, we strongly encourage LGBTQ2SIA+, Indigenous, and writers of colour to submit their work.

Invisible Publishing is also home to the Bibliophonic series of music books and the Throwback series of CanLit reissues.

If you'd like to know more, please get in touch: info@invisiblepublishing.com

Invisible